Tales from Pareidolia

Tales from Pareidolia

Stuart F Taylor

First published in 2012
Chain Bear Publishing
2 Marble House, Old Homesdale Road, Bromley, London, BR2 9JL

www.stuartftaylor.co.uk

ISBN-13: 978-0-9571646-0-4

For Mum, Dad and Lauren

Contents

Old Testament

The Gardens of Life

There was once a boy called Sembrato, who grew up in a rusty-brown land. All about him was the freshly turned soil of the earth, reaching out from below his feet and following the undulations of the hills and valleys till it met the sky at the horizon. As soon as he could walk on his own feet without tumbling, he was given a bag of seed and told to follow the pull of the plough. So, while the sun shone, he walked in the furrows of the plough and scattered his seeds in its wake.

If he felt the pangs of hunger, Sembrato was allowed to dip into the seeds from his bag. When he gasped with thirst, he could share in the rainwater that the bucketeers collected. And so, Sembrato and the rest of his people moved forward in their thousands over those hills and valleys, ploughing, sowing and raking. They never looked back to the impregnated earth, only forward to the fresh soil yet to be tilled.

One day, when the thick clouds had splintered beneath the sun and spilled its honey rays in gentle cascade, Sembrato asked his father: 'Father, why must we forever till this broken earth? What becomes of the seeds we plant? Can't we ever turn back to see?'

And Father said, 'This is how life is for us Brown Earthers. We turn the earth, we sow our seed and we move on; that is our purpose.'

'But what if we yearn for more, Father? What if we want to build, or play, or dream?'

'That is not for us, dear Son,' Father responded. 'You mustn't hunger beyond your reason. Our life here does not matter; it is the sowing of the seed that matters. Our death here does not matter; the life of the seed matters. After we die here, we will be reborn in a more beautiful place. So, if you find yourself disenchanted: think not of this Brown World, but think of the Green World that awaits all of us beyond death.'

So Sembrato, buoyed with hope, nodded and continued to sow seeds over the land and beyond the horizon. And when he became a father, he passed down his seed bag and lifted the plough. And when his children were old enough to sow, he became a raker. And when he died, the others knew to bury him so that he might enrich the soil for the seeds they'd sow and never reap. They spent a moment thinking of how they would meet him again in the Green World, before moving on to plough the untouched lands ahead.

Sembrato awoke once more as a screaming, bloody baby. In this life, his parents named him Nourris and dressed him in orange.

And when Nourris was old enough to walk in the Green World, he was given a watering can so that he might quench the earth, alongside his fellow Greens who bore hoes and pesticides. They walked forever forwards, for the crops that longed for their care grew out and over the curve of the horizon. After many years of walking and watering, Nourris grew restless and so he turned to his mother in earnest:

'Mother, these crops go on forever and ever; people are born and die as we continue to care for them. Is this all we will ever do? What more is there for us in this world?'

And Mother said, 'Son, we live on this Green World to keep these plants healthy. That is the very meaning of our being; it is why we are here.'

'But what about us, Mother, and the things that we want?'

'Son, you misunderstand our place. We are not important. We serve a greater purpose than our own desires and that's all you need to know.'

But Nourris seemed dissatisfied.

'Our time will come, son,' Mother assured him. 'After we die here, we will be reborn in the Yellow World. Life and death here mean nothing, so you would do well not to shame us with your chagrin.'

So Nourris quieted himself and returned to the crops that would busy him forever. Through his relatively long life, he watered and dusted, hoed and sprayed and though he passed many millions of young plants, each of which looked the same and none of which returned a favour. He raised children of his own and died alone, as all Green Worlders are wont to do.

And, just as he was promised, he was born again in the world of yellow. He was named Sasin and he worked with his parents to harvest the ripened crops from the infinite fields of fruit, seed and vegetable. Oh, they piled high the stacks of harvest along the rocky roads that ran through the fields, taking only what they needed to survive. The days were long and the work was hard and Sasin watched with curiosity the blank, bored faces of the crowds working the harvest.

'Father,' he asked, 'why do we work so endlessly and tirelessly in these fields? Whom do we harvest for? Where do the stone roads lead? Is there anything beyond the fruit?'

'Ah Sasin,' Father said, 'we do no ask questions such as these. We have harvested for all the generations in hearsay's memory, as it was told by my mother to me and her mother to her and so on, back to a time we cannot know. Our lives are for reaping and not for questioning.'

'But in my head, I have a thousand questions to ask - and a thousand more still brewing.'

'Then silence those questions, young Sasin. For the harder we work, the quicker we shall die; the quicker we die, the sooner we shall be reborn in paradise. Now hush, be diligent, and work as best befits a strong young boy like you.'

So Sasin kept his eager mind at bay, chastised his questioning mind and put his efforts to reaping, living as his father taught him. He grew tall and strong, but the work was tough and a mere decade after the birth of his daughter, his body gave in and he died an exhausted, peaceful death, waiting for another world.

He did indeed awake once more. He grew up in the kind support of his parents, reading books and drawing pictures, watching the sky roll by and the birds turn and flock as if they were one being; feeling the leaves turn crisp and brown in autumn before abandoning the tree altogether. One day, when he was two heads shorter than a full-grown man, he wandered out of his little red brick house and into the garden, where his Mother was sitting in the sunshine, scrawling notes in the margin of a book.

'Mother, what is the purpose of life?' young Nolan asked (for Nolan was his name in this life).

'Why, whatever do you mean, Nolan?' said Mother.

'Our purpose? Why are we here? Why do we exist?'

'Why ever would we need a purpose? What is so inadequate about being alive that you need a purpose also?'

'I feel a need for a purpose, Mother, for a reason to be.'

'Dearest Nolan, my sweet boy.' Mother cradled his head in her gentle fingers. 'You must find your own purpose. Life comes around but once, so you must make the very best of it.'

'You mean, when I die, I'm gone forever?'

'We've never known any different, my love. Why would you think anything else?'

'So I can do whatever I wish?'

'As long as you don't spoil it for anyone else – why not?'

'Anything I wish...'

And after many years of soul-searching, Nolan set himself to architecture. He studied the great art for a long decade and came to create some of the largest, grandest buildings the world had ever known. He spent his life building taller and more wondrous places for people to live, work and play. He inspired all those who saw his buildings to reach their own great heights, just as he had. And the people long spoke the tale of the boy who aspired to be great and made it so, and the tale was passed on, beyond the lives of those who told it and to all those who aspired to greatness.

The Speciation Song

Lizard in the grass,
She likes to catch the 'hoppers,
She runs and darts so fast,
So no one ever stops 'er.
Lizard in the grass,
Coloured green to match the meadow,
'Er belly hangs real low,
And hides 'er from the sparrow.

But things can't stay the same,
And the world around 'er changes,
In tiny little steps,
'Er body rearranges.
In a million years she'll wake,
As a lizard by the lake.

Lizard by the lake,
She likes to eat the fishes,
'Er lungs she can inflate,
So she dives in as she wishes.
Lizard by the lake,
'Er toes with webs are sealed,
Swimmin' like a snake,
With 'er tail that's like an eel's.

But things can't stay the same,
And the world around 'er changes,
In tiny little steps,
'Er body rearranges.
In a million years she'll be,
A lizard of the tree.

Lizard of the tree,
'Er legs are strong for scalin',
Leapin' limb to limb
With armpit wings, she's sailin'.
Lizard of the tree,
For eggs, 'er mouth is wider,
The birds, they look for she,
But 'er mottled skin, it hides 'er.

But the lizard of the lake,
And the lizard in the tree,
The daughters, they are both,
Of the grass lizard, you see.
One went east, the other west,
Put them bodies to the test.

From the lizard in the grass,
Their own paths they have come by,
The one's become a swimmer,
The other's learned to fly.
And while they share their old grandmother,
They are strangers to each other!

The Speciation Song

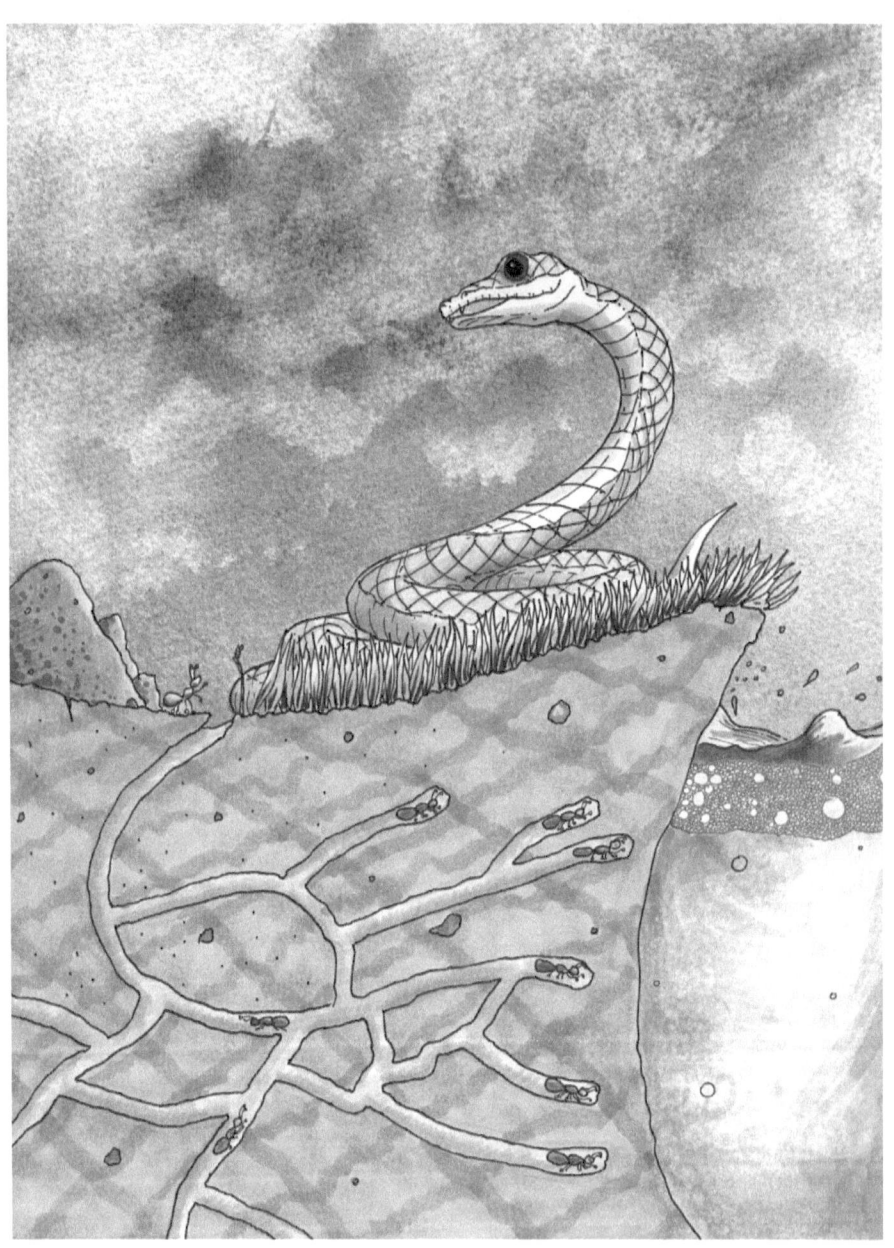

The Snake and the Ant

There is a fast-churning confluence down where that big, thundering river meets the skinny one. If you were to go down to the grass near where the waters touch the land, you'll see all sorts of little holes there in the ground. That is where the ants live – right down in the little holes. And if you listen real close, you can hear their little chant:

> *'So we dig, so we dig,*
> *Like an ant surely should,*
> *Move the earth, move the earth,*
> *For an ant's life is good.'*

Well those ants sure loved to dig. You'd think it was all they cared about. As the generations rolled by, their colony grew, bringing need for more and more space right there in the underground. As luck would have it, more ants meant more digging and so the solution to their trouble was obvious: why, they'd dig themselves more room. Oh, how they dug. If you could see their little arms working, you'd be witness to nothing but a blur of ants and shifting dirt.

Well, one particular cloudy day, a little ant was carrying her dirt clump up and out of the underground to toss it out of sight. When she finally emerged into the bright daylight, she saw a great, winding snake right there in the grass.

'Hello there, little ant,' said the Snake. 'What brings you up here with the surface dwellers?'

'I'm digging a tunnel, Snake,' said the Ant. 'As soon as I am done with this clump, I can go on down and dig some more.'

'I hear your kind digging underground,' said the Snake, for it was well known that snakes spent their days with their heads to the ground and heard every little vibration that passed on by. 'Why is it that you ants only dig eastwise and never westwise?'

'Eastwise is where the clay dirt lies, Snake. Westwise is thick with chalky dirt. We only ever dig in the clay dirt.'

'Why ever's that?'

'That's the way digging is done, Snake.'

'Did you know that further eastwise runs a raging river?' said the Snake. 'If you keep digging and digging, you'll be washed away for sure.'

'We ain't never tried digging in the chalky dirt and we won't waste good digging time trying it now, thank you, Snake.'

'Suit yourself, Ant,' said the Snake, coiling himself up for a snooze in the sun.

And the Ant went back down under the earth and joined in the chorus:

'So we dig, so we dig,
Like an ant surely should,
Move the earth, move the earth,
For an ant's life is good.'

The very next day, the little Ant was once again carrying a big old clump of dirt out to the surface when she saw the Snake gliding by.

'Hello there, little Ant,' said the Snake. 'Still digging eastwise, I hear.'

'Good day to you, Snake,' said the Ant. 'As I told you, we only ever dig eastwise: right on into the clay dirt.'

'And as I told you, you are still digging towards a raging river,' said the Snake.

He flickered his tongue right out, real fast. If you tried to flick your tongue out of your mouth as fast as you could, I promise you'd be a great deal slower than the Snake. 'Why not go and take a look for yourself?'

The Ant looked eastwise and said, 'I don't see anything but dirt and grass, Snake.'

'That is because you are small and slight, little Ant,' said the Snake, rising up on his long back. 'If you could make yourself tall like me, you would see it for sure.'

'Well I will always be an ant and carry my smallness with me. I cannot see a river,' said the Ant.

'Perhaps if you were to sit-a-seat on my nose I could show it to you,' said the Snake.

'I cannot waste good time riding on your nose, thank you, Snake'

'Suit yourself, Ant.'

And the Ant returned to the underground and joined the jolly chorus:

'So we dig, so we dig,
Like an ant surely should,
Move the earth, move the earth,
For an ant's life is good.'

The third day came and, once again, the little Ant took her clump of dirt up to the surface. And out there in the autumn-red sunshine was the Snake again, lazing in the grass, his head to the earth.

'I hear you still dig-digging eastwise.'

'So we do, Snake,' said the Ant. 'And so we will.'

'You're awful close to that river now. I say it won't be long till that water comes flooding in and sweeps you all away. I still say it's best to turn on westwise towards the chalky dirt that stretches on for all the dry miles you'll ever need.'

'Snake, come now,' said the Ant. 'Everyone knows you're as villainous as they come. Why, you swallow beasts whole and melt them in your bloated body - as awful a thing as I've ever heard. I wish you'd say no more!'

'That may be so, that may be faux; but eat mice or kill mice, I won't move the river away. I fare you well, little Ant.'

'Our time spent talking is time spent not digging, Snake. You can keep your farewells and leave me be.'

And the little ant returned to her fellows in the clay dirt, where they surely did sing:

'So we dig, so we dig,
Like an ant surely should,
Move the earth, move the earth,
For an ant's life is good.'

And on the fourth day, the Snake did not speak to the little Ant. This was partly because those heedless ants had dug on through to that raging river and flooded themselves away, and partly because he had swallowed a whole mongoose.

Stained Glass Windows

Once upon a year, the Old King and his Young Queen at last sired an heir: a baby boy. They named him Gullifer. Now, the winter that year was particularly cold, freezing the river to glass and frosting the grass white. The King, in his elderly age, succumbed to the bitter weather and, in the nation's mourning, Gullifer became the infant King.

The palace hung all of its attention on the young and vulnerable King Gullifer. The Queen, in her youth, was terrified that a tragedy might befall her child and deprive the Kingdom of an heir. The nation was in deep tension with surrounding lands and the fear of war was growing, and so, deep in paranoia, she secreted herself and the baby away in the highest chamber of the palace. This chamber once stood as a chapel, and so it was that Gullifer grew up warmed by the bright, coloured light from the tall shapes and ancient saints of the stained glass windows.

Back in the days when the Young Queen was courting the Old King, she had fallen for his warm charm and wicked wit. When he presented her with fine embroidered dresses, dined her with succulent foods and showed her his vast riches, it had never occurred to her to be curious of the origin of this wealth. She had been raised in the shrewdness of gift horses, after all. But once she became the guardian of the monarch, she learned that the royal clothes were crafted by the hands of slaves, the food was slaughtered and cooked in the long hours of servants, and the gold piled up from the overtaxed paupers. Knowing this disturbed her sensibilities, though she hardened her resolve to watch over her child and grant him a peaceful life. As she looked down on her sleeping infant through the blur of melancholy, she vowed to keep him from this terrible knowledge. Nothing should ever break his rosy innocence.

King Gullifer knew from a very young age that he would be at the helm of his vast country when he grew up. As soon as he could stand he would press his soft, pink face against the yellows and blues and reds of the stained glass window. It was his only portal from the isolation of the chapel. His cheeks mashed cold to the glass as he looked through at the land that rolled out to the horizon.

'Is that field mine?' he asked.

'Of course,' the Queen said.

'Is that river mine?' he asked.

'Of course,' the Queen said.

'And the forest, too?'

'Everything you can see is yours, son.'

And King Gullifer was increasingly curious in his youth, as expected from one confined to a single room. He asked the Queen every question on his mind about the world and, to satisfy his thirst, the Queen summoned visiting scholars and professors to teach him the ways of the world. But she warned them never to tell him about the darker aspects of the Kingdom; the expense at which his fortunes came.

One day, young King Gullifer was being dressed by his handmaidens when he turned to the Queen and asked:

'Mother, where do clothes come from?'

'That is a good question,' the Queen said, without pause. 'To summon your clothing, your handmaidens walk down to the river and they ask the heavens for clothing and jewellery for their King. Then, your clothes are sent down the river and collected by the maidens.'

The maidens looked at one another, but did not speak. Gullifer was satisfied, for this made him feel special. He looked after his heaven-sent clothes with great affection.

A month by, young King Gullifer was eating a delicious meal by candlelight. He looked up from the pork joint, potatoes cabbage and gravy and asked:

'Mother, where do meals come from?'

'That is an interesting question,' the Queen said. 'You see, Gullifer, every morning, noon and eve, the chef leaves the palace and goes to a great tree in a meadow. There he stands before the tree and asks it pleasantly for food fit for a king. The tree then lowers a branch with a full plate of food - nutritious, steaming-hot and ready to eat.'

And the young King was satisfied, for he very much liked the story of where his food came from.

Another month by, the Queen was teaching Gullifer the rules of numbers, using gold coins from his vault of riches. Looking over the piles of gold, Gullifer asked:

'Mother, where does all my gold come from?'

'That's a good question,' said the Queen. 'You see, if you think of money before you go to sleep at night, then the Gold Pixie will bring you more coins by morning. The longer you sleep, the more coins you will receive.'

And the King was most content. That night he slept longer and more peacefully that any nights before, though so vast were his riches that he could not detect a difference in the morning.

And so it continued. The Queen filled Gullifer's head with knowledge whilst keeping him safe from the terrible truths that most haunted her.

After many years, the King grew to be a young man, with curly locks on his head and wisps of a beard on his chin. He was preparing to ascend to his throne and, after many years of patience in the ever-claustrophobic chambers, sit at the head of the Kingdom. He itched to move from behind the colours of the stained glass windows.

Most unfortunately, on the day of his coronation, war finally broke upon the land. The Kingdom was attacked by a mighty, invading army. The army rose from the southern border and charged towards the capital, leaving town after burning town in its dusty wake. The Kingdom, at peace for so long, was unprepared. As the approaching enemy reached the city walls, King Gullifer's soldiers took the King to his carriage and told the horse driver to take him far, far from danger. As the carriage set off, a great catapult hit the highest tower of the palace and the coloured stained glass rained down upon King and carriage. *Yah!* - the coach driver sped the carriage away! As the King looked back on the burning palace, he knew with sadness that his mother had not been granted the luxury of escape. Jolting with the memories of her warm embrace, her evening stories and her struggle to turn him into a king, he shed a quiet tear. But, as King, he knew it to be the only tear he could allow himself, and it soon evaporated into the warm afternoon air.

After many, many miles of bumpy and frantic escaping, the coach driver stopped at a cross in the roads. He told the King that he was compelled to return to the palace so that he might try and save his family, but he would leave the King here where it was safe. The King, in his benevolence and naivety, alighted and bid him good fortune, taking a shard of stained glass from the canopy of the carriage and planting it in the pocket at his breast.

He was at an intersection of four prairies. He looked across the landscape and realised that, for the first time in his life, he could see the world in its full spectrum. He saw pale blues break against deep greens, yellows bursting from the earthy reds. Beauty stretched out in every direction, further than any distance he'd ever imagined. He decided that he would cross the lands and try to find a hamlet where he might find respite. He trekked for a day and a half across the undulating grounds – so tiring it was! Taking the shard of stained glass from his pocket, he held it before his eyes. How limiting that window had been! He passed strange animals, plodding lazily in the grass. Some were tall, sleek and muscular; others were small and fluffed white; yet more were large, bulky beasts with horns. How magical they all were. They bade him due reverence as he passed, a dopey serenity hanging from their faces. Shapes darted across the air, too quick for him to discern. Strange chirping songs harked and larked from every direction. How busy, this tranquillity!

He reached the outskirts of a hamlet in the late afternoon hours. The cottages there followed the curve of a freshwater brook that chattered over smooth stones. The King assessed himself: the journey had soiled his robes deeply with mud, sweat and grass.

'I need new garments to present myself to my people,' Gullifer thought. Standing at the water's edge, he remembered what his mother had told him and looked skywards:

'Heavens, I ask you to present me with new clothing so that I may stand before my people as their King.'

He wasn't sure what was supposed to happen next. He waited. He asked again. How long did the garment take to journey the river, he wondered. Perhaps this was a particularly long stream. He asked again, on his knees. He was interrupted by a voice:

'Mister Man, what are you doing?'

A young maiden in a grey dress stood before him, straight-backed and wide-eyed. Her tawny hair fell to her hips, where it was burned gold by the sun. Her hands met at her front and she swayed on her heels.

'Young Lady, I am asking the heavens for clothes. I cannot walk within my Kingdom in such filthy rags,' said Gullifer.

'Kingdom? But, Mister Man, this is a Kingdom no more – it is an Empire, now Emperor Mallessandro is in charge.'

'So quickly my Kingdom has fallen?'

'And that's not how you get clothing,' the maiden continued. 'You have to make it yourself. You can take the woolly coat from a sheep,' she pointed to a sheep, 'and spin it into wool and knit it into clothing. That is one way.'

'That sounds far too ridiculous. My clothes always come quickly and in abundance. It would take forever to make clothes that way, silly lady.'

'Please, Mister Man, but my grandfather was enslaved by the palace for many decades. He spent half his life making royal clothing.'

'That sounds obscene.' Gullifer stood, his fists to his hips. 'I would never steal the coat from a sheep and enslave a man to turn it to robes! What has happened here is that the river knows I am no longer King, so it will not provide me with royal garb. No matter!'

And Gullifer decided to enter the village as an equal in shabby clothes. He badly needed a roof above his head. He decided to knock at the doors of the village dwellers, and as an offering he would bring them a wonderful feast. So he headed to the largest tree he could see in the meadow of sheep and raised his hands, open.

'Oh great tree! Won't you pass me food fit for those generous enough to shelter me?'

The maiden giggled from the stone wall at the edge of the field, kicking her ankle with her heel. The tree was not generous in response.

'Tell me, maiden,' Gullifer asked, 'do all trees give out meals or are there particular ones I need to seek out?'

'Trees don't give out meals, Mister Man,' the maiden laughed.

'I tell you, they do. All of my meals were gifted by trees.'

'I can tell you how to make a good meal, if you like,' said the maiden, skipping over to him. And she recalled all her favourite meals – roast beef, mashed potato, onion soup and buttered bread, steak and kidney pie... She detailed the grotesqueries supporting each meal – the slaughtering of livestock and the harvesting of its parts, the tearing of vegetables from the ground, the boiling and slicing, the plucking of spices from flowers, the grinding of flour and all the many subtle labours of cuisine.

The young King was shocked. Butchering animals? Chicken that came from chickens? Potatoes that lived in the dirt? And oh – the great effort! None of it made any sense at all!

'Young maiden, I fear you are quite, quite mad!' Gullifer rubbed his temples and closed his eyes. She made everything outside of his tall chamber sound so unnecessarily difficult and disturbing.

'You are silly, Mister Man!' the maiden tutted. She grabbed his hand, leading him out of the field. 'Come, you can stay with my family, I'm sure.'

And she took him to her home where he was warmly welcomed by her mother, father and brother. Supper was being made. Curious, the King thought to himself. So one *could* make meals the laborious way! They must not have heard of the generosity of trees, whose limbs perhaps bowed only to royalty.

They ate and made easy conversation. When he told them he was their King, they responded politely. He knew they did not believe him – after all, he had never before been in public; no one knew his face.

They gave him a space to sleep. As he settled to doze, he vowed to repay their generosity so he made a little wish to the Gold Pixie and drifted to sleep on the hard floor. But when he awoke, there was no gold to be seen! Had the new Emperor destroyed the Gold Pixie? Gullifer addressed the family:

'Kind people, I meant to repay you for all your good heartedness. But when I wished to the Gold Pixie, she brought me no gold. I feel most humbled and small, with nothing to give.'

'Mister Man,' the maiden wagged her finger as her family stared, bemused. 'You cannot simply wish for gold. You have to earn it. For our gold we work the land, tend to our animals and sell the bounty at market.'

'Then that I shall do for you!' the King said, again, curious as to why people chose such a complicated route to a wishable outcome. 'I will work on your land and raise your animals so that you may find your wealth at market.'

And so the King worked the land of the family and he kept the animals healthy and strong. And, in this manner, Gullifer became as one of the family. After a few years, he and the maiden fell in love and were happily wed and inherited the land. They worked hard to support their own family, even making their own clothing, as the maiden once taught.

And every day Gullifer, who wore a pendant he has fashioned from his shard of stained glass, still returned to the brook and to the tree; there he asked for clothes and food; he continued to wish for riches from his bed at night. Through seasons passing, as his hair grew thin and white, never did a day pass without this ritual.

When they were old and lying in bed on the last day of their life, the maiden turned to Gullifer and said:

'My dear Mister Man, every day you work hard to help earn our living, grow our food and make our clothing. You've seen everything I've told you about life to be true. And yet you always kept to your funny old ways. Why was that?'

'My love,' Gullifer said, 'I asked for clothing and I am clothed; I asked for food and I ate; I asked for wealth and I earned it. Everything followed as I expected.'

And she smiled at him and lay her head on his chest. And with her last breath, before she could stop herself, she whispered, 'That's silly, Mister Man.'

And there they lay forever.

Stained Glass Windows

Two Sisters on the Road to Grandfafa

There were once two sisters named Vittie and Pansy who were travelling to their grandfather's house, way out in the west. They had never journeyed there alone before but they were finally old enough to be trusted out in the wide, wide world. Their father had told them over and again simply to follow the old road all the way from east to west. Their grandfather lived in the only red house in the western village.

So the two sisters wound their way down the old road, round the hills and through the mists. Vittie was a hint of a shade taller and let her blonde hair grow long and wavy; Pansy had cut her hair to a bob to keep her hair from catching in the longest twigs when she went tree-climbing. Both bearing dark brown eyes and a smattering of cheek freckles, they might be indistinguishable were it not for the way they wore their faces – Vittie with a pout and Pansy with a snarl. They skipped down the old road, although not in step – Vittie favoured her left foot and Pansy, her right.

Before long, they came upon a fork in the road. The left road meandered gently over shallow dales while the right road zagged into some dark woods.

'Fafa didn't tell us 'bout no fork in the road,' said Vittie.

'Which way d'you think we ought to go?' asked Pansy.

'Well all I see is the left road looks all hells easier than that scary looking right road,' said Vittie.

'But that don't make it the road to Grandfafa,' said Pansy. 'Maybe we should be going back to ask Fafa again, to be sure.'

'Nah, I ain't going' back. We can't be lookin' like fools, and besidin' that – we won't get to Grandfafa till all kinds of darkness. I'm off down the left path.'

'Well, I don't wanna go the wrong way,' said Pansy. 'I'm gonna hold here till I can work out which road is right.'

So Vittie skipped off down the left path and Pansy sat at the divide, all a-wondering which way she should turn. She looked leftways and rightways but neither gave a clue. Then, all of an instant, the sun punched its way out of the clouds and shone out over the misty landscape. Pansy hid her eyes from its dazzle and remembered that it was afternoon times. And in the afternoon times, the sun would be heading west for the evening. Well, wouldn't you know it – the west was exactly where the right path went, so she skipped her way all through those scary woods. Though the wooded path was hung with spindled branches and sleeping bats, she was glad that it shielded her from the red glare of the setting sun. With a dance in her gait, she made her way to the village where her grandfather lived.

When she got to the village, she decided to wait by the old stone well for her sister to arrive. She couldn't turn up to her grandfather's house without Vittie – she'd surely worry him halfway to death! Where's your sister at, he'd say. I do scare so that she's horribly hurt! Perhaps he'd scold Pansy for letting Vittie wander the wilderness alone; he was all too keen to wag his finger at the best of times. So she waited and waited, and it got dark and cold in the sun's neglect, forcing her to pull down her sleeves and bundle her body all up tight on the ground at the foot of the well. After a long, long time, Vittie finally appeared from a dark road out from the shadowy part of town. Why, she was shivering, wet and bedraggled like she'd been carried all the way from thither to hither by a tornado.

'What's gone and happened to you, sister?' said Pansy.

'Oh, sister, it was so Godawful!' said Vittie. 'First, my path went right through a swamp so I was all sopped in swamp-water up to my knickers! Then I wandered out into a plain where I happened upon a pack of roarin', scratchin', bitin' lions. Oh, they chased me – they chased me a-runnin' through a bramble thatch, they did! Cut me all to gashes! Then I saw I was in the southward village and that's when I knew I was all kinds of directions out of sorts. So I went and I climbed over rocks and boulders and ran all the way here, not stoppin', not once!'

Looking at the soaking stains upon her clothes and the bloody scores across her arms and legs, Pansy knew that Vittie had suffered for her haste and so chastised her none. Instead, she took Vittie gently by her arm and led her to the red house where their grandfather lived.

'Be careful of my cuts and scuffs, sister!' said Vittie, wincing at her touch.

Now, by this point it was very late in the night, what with Vittie's tardiness and all, so they decided to sneak into the house and save waking their Grandfafa.

'I tell you, sister,' said Vittie, as they tiptoed over the old floorboards, 'I'm all kinds of parched. I haven't had myself a drink since we left home this morning.'

'Me neither,' said Pansy. 'Let's see what Grandfafa has in the kitchen.'

So they crept into kitchen and creaked open the old refrigerator, one of those with the lights inside that lit everything up all buttery-like. There wasn't much in there, just a hunk of cheese, all wrapped in brown paper, a jar of pickled cucumbers and a large brown bottle, stoppered tight with a cork. Vittie grabbed it.

'Wait!' said Pansy.

Vittie popped the cork and gave the opening a sniff.

'It don't smell of nothin',' said Vittie.

'We don't know what it is, sister. You oughtn't drink it till you know what it is.'

'But I'm so thirsty! Why would Grandfafa keep a bottle in his refrigerator that I couldn't drink from? I want to drink now!' And she tipped back the bottle and glugged several swallows' full.

'Ugh! It tastes 'orrible!' Vittie gagged and choked. Still coughing and spluttering, she collapsed to her hands and spluttered scarlet all over the kitchen floor.

'It's poison, you silly sister!' yelled Pansy!

'Fix it! Get me medicine!' rasped Vittie, her eyes turning yellow.

And Pansy rushed about the kitchen, flipping open cupboard after cupboard. She saw tall condiments and stacked plates, wine goblets and biscuit tins. Vittie rolled a-frantic on the floor; her veins swelled green and her ears wept wax. Pansy fought through the cupboards until finally she saw a red medicine box all sitting all alone on a shelf. She yanked it out by its little red handle but its weight surprised her and she dropped it. Hitting the side with a metallic clang, it scattered the medicines within all over the floor: bright pills, round pills, needles, salves and syrups. Pansy danced a panic – which to choose?

Vittie reached out and grabbed a square, pink pill.

'No, sister!' warned Pansy.

'But I'm dying!' barked Vittie. And she popped that pink pill right into her mouth and swallowed.

Well, no one would know what might have happened but, as very good fortune would have it, that little pill pulled from a jumbled assortment stopped the choking right there and then. Vittie lay back on the kitchen floor. The yellowness in her eyes faded, her face stopped leaking and her body stilled. She was thoroughly exhausted, but well.

'Are you okay, sister?' asked Pansy.

'Yes, of course,' said Vittie. 'Pink never done me no harm before, and it never will.'

'You were very, very lucky, hasty sister,' said Pansy.

'What are you talkin' about, "lucky"?' said Vittie. 'I'm nothin' but a genius, is what I am.'

Ignoring Pansy's indignant scowl, Vittie dusted herself off and headed to bed, remembering only her oh-so-supreme judgement in the face of a crisis. She trotted upstairs, hopped over the creaky stair and ducked under the low beam, despite the darkness. She chuckled at her genius – if only her sister could be as skilled as she. She reached the hallway at the top of the stairs and was struck disoriented by the night's darkness. Which room was hers? She hadn't stayed the night in oh-so-long. But then she saw a beam of moonlight, caught through the leaves of the tree by the window. Its light was shaped to a heart and landed on the far most door. It was a sign! Vittie skipped to the end of the hallway and hopped into the bedroom to find... Grandfafa and Esmendina, the old lady from the sweet shop! They were naked, all bundled on top of one another, grabbing and kissing and – oh no! Vittie shut the door and ran back downstairs at once: two steps, three steps at a time, until she was down in the sitting room and curled up tight under a great blanket where she spent the rest of the night.

Little Boy Prophet

Little Boy Prophet

There once was a boy who lived in a wooden house, in a bendy street of wooden houses, in a town of bendy streets. He was called Herbert the Sherbet, for his father was a confectioner and his mother a lover of rhyme. But that is neither here nor there.

One autumnal day, Herbert was out playing marbles beneath the silver-barked maple tree, when the tree shed a rusty leaf that tumbled clumsily through the air and onto his knee. Not a second later, he heard his mother call him from the house for tea. As Herbert began to gather his marbles into their pouch, another maple leaf fell and, a moment later, his mother called again.

'That's weird,' thought Herbert. 'I wonder if a leaf falls once more, will my mother call again also?'

He waited a few moments and, as a breeze passed by, a third leaf fell and his mother called again – this time in a heated voice, for she had already called once and twice. As Herbert tucked into his dinner of peas and mash, he began to wonder about the way the world might be woven together. Could the tiniest tug on one thread affect the other threads in that great tapestry? This could be something very special indeed, he thought, so he decided to pay special attention to all the goings-on around him.

He bought himself a notebook – a leather-bound one that would keep from damage – and he inked in all of the things he saw as the world passed by. He watched the moon and the sun and the stars; his parents, his friends and his teachers; the leaves, the horses and the winds. He watched everything that did a thing, to see what happened after.

Eventually, his leather-bound notebook was filled with his frantic writings. He'd been watching so long that he found he could start predicting by instinct alone, allowing the world to twist and shape his thoughts into premonitions. He wasn't always right, of course, but the accuracy of some of his predictions began to frighten him a little. On a swell of confidence, he decided to bring his gift before his mother and father.

'Mother, Father,' he said. 'I can tell you the future. I have read the world and it's telling me that, tomorrow, I shall get a poor mark in school, it will rain all afternoon and mother will have a terrible fall.'

His father laughed away young Herbert's predictions with a boisterous mussing of his hair but his mother became worried. What had Herbert meant by a terrible fall? She hardly slept a wink that night thinking about it. All the next day she tip-toed around the house, minding every step and every hazard like it might be the end of her. But, because she was so aware of her each and every step, she became unbalanced when the bright afternoon sun caught her eye. She tumbled down the stairs, bashing her poor behind to a great purple swelling. Father was quite astonished. If only he had taken heed of Herbert the Sherbet, then Mother would not be fixed up in bed with an oversized blackcurrant for a bottom.

'You've a gift, my boy,' said Father. 'It's a gift we must share with the world.'

So Herbert's father led him to the old town hall, where he presented Herbert to the folks at the weekly town meeting. Herbert had never been to the hall before and he was awed by its magnificence. Its tall ceilings were supported by a great network of wooden beams, criss-crossing their way down its length, meeting at the white, umbrella-like pillars that divided the rows of red wooden chairs. The windows were tall and let the sunlight bounce over the white walls, lighting up the space like winter. These meetings were the week's special event, so the people had come dressed in all their formal finery: tall hats, shiny shoes, buttoned dresses and the like. While Herbert waited on the stage, looking out to the rows and rows of townsfolk, he felt his knees bounce from the ball of his foot as the nerves took hold. His father gave him a grand introduction and called him a gifted forward-seer and one of the most important individuals to arise from their humble town. Herbert was waved forward to address the audience, his nerves partly calmed by his father's enthusiastic support.

'At the moment, I see a few shadows approaching, I do,' he said, choking back dryness. 'Someone here will come into a great deal of money, I see. Someone here will die and someone else will meet their sweetheart. All of this will come in the soon-times.'

The hall echoed with the bluster of the townsfolk. No one knew what to think, though they knew these were all exciting possibilities for quite a few of them. They weren't sure whether to believe the confectioner's son – maybe he spoke the truth, maybe not – but they all wanted to fall on the right side of fate's axe, if it fell at all. The first thing a great number of them did was to buy themselves an extra ticket for the town's popular Jumble Lottery. The second thing they did was to pick themselves a dandy bunch of flowers, in case they saw their sweetheart wander by.

At the very next town meeting, a man stood up from his seat so all could see him. Usually, he was a scruffy sort: wild-haired, with mismatched, dusty clothes and more than a patch or two on his sleeves. Today, however, he was topped and tailed in well-shaped and fitted wares that had surely been purchased that very week.

'Would you believe it?' he said, his eyes wide and white. 'Last week, I heard Herbert the Sherbet's prognostications and – not a while later – I went on down and bought myself a good handful of Jumble Lottery tickets, for something told me that old Herbert was talking about me. And what do you know? I went on to win last week's Jumble Lottery. And, when I was all done up in my new finery, I only went and met this beautiful lady beside me who henceforth agreed to be my belle!'

The crowd gasped and cheered. The little boy had seen it coming, they cried. He was blessed with a gift from goodness-knows-where and they should respect him and revere him. So Herbert the Sherbet became the famous truth-teller of that town, making himself regular at the weekly town meetings and on special occasions like the beginning of the harvest season.

A few moons passed. One particular dusk, Herbert found himself troubled by something gone awry. He was watching a bat circling the house, its darkness a flutter against the dim sky. He knew by instinct that when a bat circles your house that a thunderstorm was soon to brew. But that bat had been dizzying itself for nigh on an hour and there was no peep of a cloud, let alone a storm.

This sent his brain tumbling into confusion, so he decided to check himself in secret. He checked his observations for the day and decided to make a few simple foretellings for the morrow: his father would make eggs for breakfast, the milk dregs would turn sour and the apple tree at the end of the lane would yield its first apple of the season. He struggled to sleep that night, hoping his doubts would be dispelled.

The next day, he hopped down to the kitchen and his father was scrambling up eggs for breakfast. He tucked into them heartily and found they tasted more delicious than any eggs he'd ever eaten before. After breakfast, his mother turned to him and said, 'Oh Herbert, the milk dregs have turned sour. Will you run off to the farmer and fetch us another flask?'

Herbert skipped down the lane to the farm, singing to himself and filling with confidence. He passed the apple tree at the end of the lane and said, 'Just to be sure, on the way back I shall wait here for the first apple to fall.'

So he fetched flask of milk from the farmer and, as he promised, he stopped on his way home to wait by the apple tree. For a long time nothing happened, though the tree looked like it was straining to give its apples as the wind sent shivers through its branches. But night fell and still no apple dropped. Beneath a clear sky of stars as midnight approached, Herbert kicked the trunk of the tree to encourage any eager fruit, but none fell and he returned home. His mother gave him a great hell of a scalding for being out so long that the fresh milk had turned sour. But Herbert was more upset by the rebellion of the apple tree.

Was he losing his power? Could the mysterious source behind his gift have dried up so suddenly and unexpectedly? It was too cruel to be true. He had seen the apple falling so clearly in his mind, but the real tree chose to selfishly cling to its fruit. Perhaps he'd just been lazy and sloppy in his readings.

Despite his shaken confidence, he attended the town meeting as usual, and all the bundle of frights he was for it, too. The town hall was more packed and bustling than it had been in previous years now that Herbert the Sherbet had become the talk of the town. Though, this time, when Herbert was up there on the stage his fear and worry stifled his conviction and he was no longer sure what he saw. So he did the only thing he could: he made it up, right there on the stage. It was better than spill the truth of his worries, face the shame and lose the celebrity that strengthened him. He spoke about the weather, about people's general well-being and of visitors coming to town. He was sure something would sit right with the people and was pleased to see them absorbing his words as they had ever done.

After the town meeting was over, the Mayor of the town took Herbert, his mother and father aside and told them, 'I have a special surprise for you. I have secured a special caravan to take you from town to town to spread your fortunes, so that everyone can hear your good words and, hopefully, hear about the town the brought you up. What say you?'

Before Herbert could hesitate, his father and mother had already shaken the Mayor by the hand and dashed off to coo in admiration over the caravan. Herbert was about to go on tour.

The roads between towns were long and meandering as Herbert, his family and their caravan curled around the hills, valleys and forests. The rough, stony surface caused the caravan to sashay lazily and Herbert's stomach turned over something rotten. But it wasn't the awkward motion of the caravan that sickened him – it was the worry that he was a fraud. As the days of travelling went by, he continued to make private foretellings to himself; some came true but many more did not. He didn't understand and it drove him to despair. He yelled at Mother and Father and they scolded him for letting his fame inflate his ego. He sat in the corner of the caravan, silently twiddling broken twine between his fingers and trying to foresee something – anything. But he realised he saw the truth as often as he was mistaken and he could not understand why. He used to be so skilled, didn't he?

He tried to look backwards, rather than forwards. He tried to remember the foresights that came to pass. It began with his mother and her fall. That indeed had come to fruition, but he had also promised rain and a bad mark in school. But it had not rained – it had been fair - and his school marks were better than he'd feared, too. In all the excitement, he'd forgotten that. And then at the town hall – that man had become rich and romanced, but no one had mentioned any deaths.

How had he let those failures escape his notice? He tried to remember the other predictions over his many months in the spotlight and realised that, time after time, he'd simply not paid any attention to his mistakes and false predictions. It began to dawn on Herbert that he'd never had much talent in foresight at all. Every time he'd seen something correctly, everyone had been so excited that they'd damn near forgotten everything else.

As the caravan neared the first town of their tour, Herbert began to wonder if the life of a fraudster was all that bad. He could conjure new foretellings wherever he went and the people in the town would do what all the others had done and remember all his true foresights at the expense of his errors. Everyone would be happy and inspired and he would move on and never have to admit to his mistakes.

So he travelled onwards, becoming famed and renowned across the ways. The crowds grew larger and larger and leaned on his words with a fattening zeal. If anyone ever turned up their nose at such 'foolish shenanigry' as Herbert's prognostications, the devoted fanatics would smack them on the snout till they bled, the bastards.

Eventually the caravan arrived in a town out in the mining country. The folk there had already known Herbert was due for a visit and so had gathered to greet him in an old quarry that they'd turned into an amphitheatre. It just so happened that there was a girl in this town, a miner girl, who was just the sort to scoff at such silly things as prophesy. But she'd heard about the snout-beatings so, long before he'd arrived, she had taken a needle from her haberdashery box and sewed her lips up tight with white cotton to ensure her silence. While Herbert was out giving the crowds his future insight she snuck out to where their caravan was parked. She heard his voice echo murmurs of the moon and marriage and so-such bouncing from the amphitheatre and knew that everyone in town would be distracted. While she was alone, she coaxed a mother hippopotamus into their caravan. Hippopotamuses are furious violent beasts, but she was well trained in herding them out from the depths of the mines, where they had taken to napping.

Before Herbert the Sherbet's big sermon had ended, the miner girl unstitched the cotton from her lips and made her way down to the front of the crowd. She raised her hand and said, 'Mr Herbert, sir – I do wonder if you could look into your own future?'

'Well, Miss,' said Herbert, 'I do suspect that it will soon be time for me to be getting to my dinner.'

The crowd laughed.

'But you'd know, wouldn't you, if something terrible was destined for you?' insisted the miner girl with a little more urgency.

'Of course I would. It would be foolish of me to ignore my own fate.'

'So you would know if the winds suddenly turned against you?'

Herbert the Sherbet paused and considered the miner girl. The eyes of the thousands looked up to him, awaiting his next word.

'Young lady,' said Herbert to the miner girl who was at least a decade older than he was, 'let me look now to the clouds. See how the high clouds move slowly east, but a few dark clouds hang low and dark? This means I shall soon be lucky in love.' And Herbert winked at her and smiled.

And the miner girl knew that Herbert the Sherbet was a charlatan and so when he and his family waved goodbye to the crowd and returned to their caravan, she made no effort to stop them. As soon as they stepped into their mobile home, the hippopotamus, in all her anger, smashed their bodies into chunks and gobbled them all down like sugared candies.

The miner girl stood before the devastated masses and said, 'Look! See how he could not even see as far as five minutes ahead – not even something as conspicuous as a hippopotamus attack! He has fooled you all!'

But the people rose up angrily against the miner girl, screaming. 'You set a beast on Herbert the Sherbet! You have taken his gift from us, you nasty, spiteful girl!'

They strung the poor miner girl up by her ankles and struck her with their mining picks until she was so full of holes that the wind whistled through her.

And that's why people make the pilgrimage from Herbert's town to the old mining country and pay visit to his statue where the caravan stands, empty forevermore.

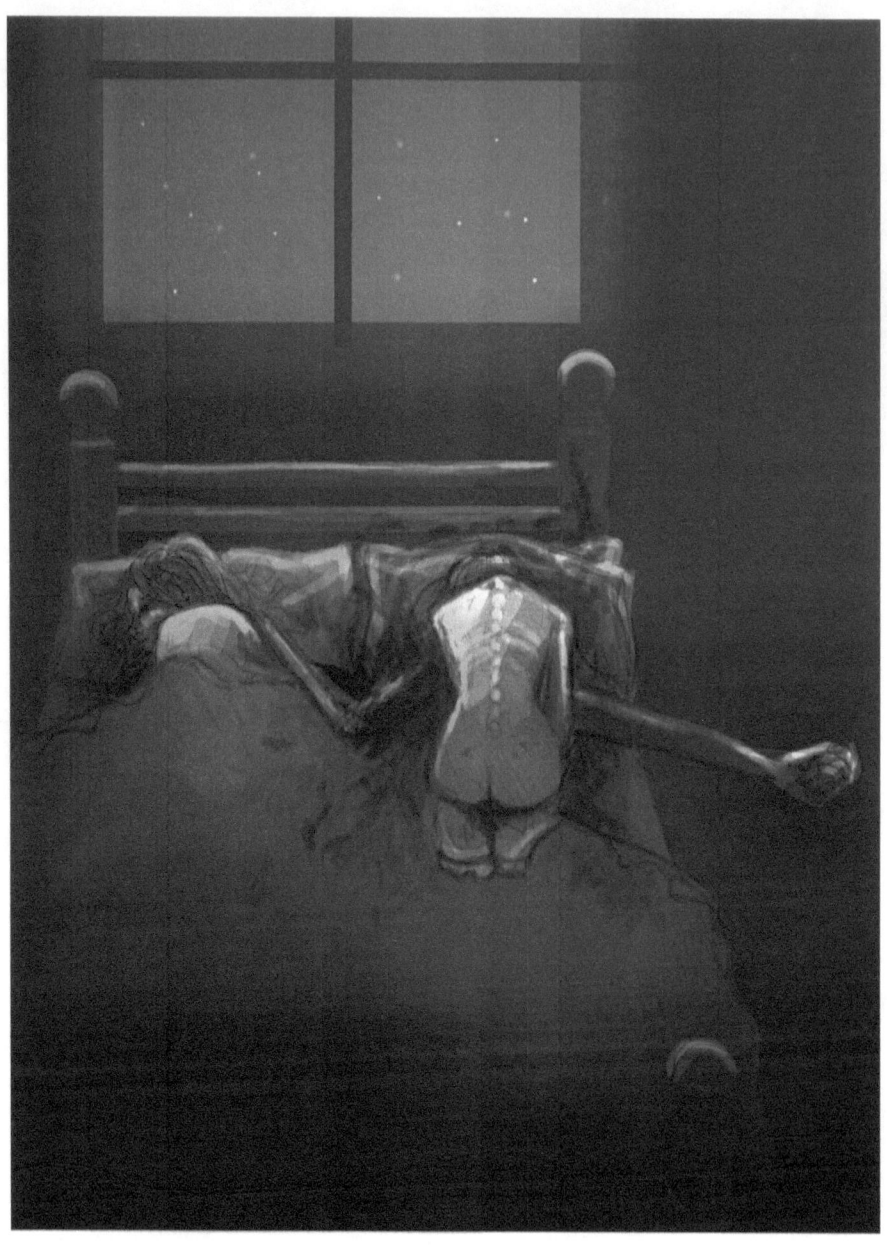

Hukommelsey

There is a sprite who lives alone in the shadows. His name is Hukommelsey. He wears the sleekest silks and satins, and his boots are finer than any made by man, with croissant toes and pyramid heels. He dines on the most delectable mushrooms and bathes in the coolest, clearest pools. These things would be a delight to any other, but Hukommelsey draws his pleasures elsewhere.

For Hukommelsey is a sadist sprite. Nothing makes him feel righter than rainbows than seeing the pain in another's eyes.

So, while by day he dines and dips and lopes and skips, by night he slinks through the slits in bedroom windows, climbing along the dark corners of your room, breaking the silence only with the patter of his toe claws. He crawls onto your bed and stands upon your sleeping belly, rising and falling with your long, snoozing breaths. At first, he likes to watch you sleep; he likes to feel he knows you.

And once his cravings spill over, he whispers a few of his magical curses and you're pinned to the bed, stuck square on your back. He'll wake you with a slap to the face and stare at you with his wrinkled, yellow crescent grin breaking the folds of his sandy skin. His faint pupils fix you with their milky, marble eyes as he turns his head this way and that, making you wait and wonder in horror.

And while you're fixed in place and wide awake, he'll poke and stab you, enough for you to feel the hot redness of your blood spill all around you; he'll twist you and bend you in shapes that will make your body will fiercely protest; he'll burn and freeze you, and chip away at the hardened flesh; he'll cut you and cleave you and show you your missing pieces; he'll poison and choke you until your insides burn and break. He'll giggle while you writhe inside, wishing for the peace of death. He'll smile when you moan and cry, lick the tears from your eyes and the spit from your mouth; he'll rub the hair from your head and the skin from your bones.

But when dawn approaches and you are broken – bloody, torn apart and frozen – he'll stitch you back and fix you up. His stitches are magic, not needle and thread: you'll bear no scars, you'll feel no ills. By sunrise you'll be just as right as when it first set. And as a final gift, Hukommelsey will vanish away your memories of the night. You'll never know he came to visit – not in feelings buried in the long-forgotten, not as a lost dream beyond your grasp – you'll be cleaned and scrubbed of all you shared that night. Hukommelsey will be gone forever from your mind, you'll wake up tired but alive.

And that is how Hukommelsey smiles, his conscience as clear as your memory. For as you only move forward, not back, that night from you he borrowed, not stole. He watches you grow into fathers and mothers; you fulfil your dreams and fight your battles as well as you would without him.

And you'll never know that for a few dark hours, Hukommelsey claimed you for his own.

Hukommelsey

Little Mouse Whiskey

In the old country kitchen of a big brick house, there sat a mouse-hole, gnawed into the yellow-white skirting board near the kitchen floor. One day, Little Mouse Whiskey poked his little pink nose out from the darkness of this mouse-hole – just a fraction – and wiggled and wiggled it till a fresh, wondrous scent warmed his insides like the flame of a hot air balloon. Not that Little Mouse Whiskey had ever seen or heard of anything as big and bold as a hot air balloon – the comparison is for you, dear reader.

'Mother Sasli, Mother Sasli!' cried Little Mouse Whiskey. 'What is that wonderful smell out there in the kitchen's air?'

Mother Sasli scampered to the opening and paused beside Little Mouse Whiskey. Her silvering fur caught the eleven o' clock sunshine and gleamed, as might an angel or a ghost. She raised her learned old nose to the air and sniffed. 'That is the smell of cheese, Little Mouse Whiskey – a dangerous smell. You must never pursue it – it exists only to entice you into a trap and kill you. That is how your Great Fathermice, Ernold and Mathieu, met their end: in the jaws of a trap.'

Mother Sasli pottered back into the mouse-hole and reached into an enclave hidden in the back wall and retrieved a severed, desiccated old mouse arm. 'See here: this is your Great Fathermouse Ernold's arm. See the old cheese scrapings in his claws? The arm was all we could save of him when we tried to pull him free.'

Horrified at the sight of what remained of his Great Fathermouse, Little Mouse Whiskey did not follow the smell, but so alluring was its savour that he sat at the edge of the mouse-hole, drinking in its sweetness through his pink, wiggling nostrils.

Why, who should appear at the mouse-hole but Iyagi the Kitchencat. Fat as a sack of potatoes and striped like fire, he was, with big yellow eyes that smiled, gentle and kind.

'Good afternoon, Little Mouse Whiskey,' said Iyagi the Kitchencat, with a gentle bow of his head. 'Mmmmm, do you smell the whiff of cheese in the air?'

'I do, Kitchencat, I do,' said Little Mouse Whiskey. 'But Mother Sasli has warned me that the smell is a trick with which to trap me, for sure!'

'Trap you? Oh, goodness gracious, no!' said Iyagi the Kitchencat. He seemed shocked by the notion. 'Whoever told you that must mean to steal the cheese for themselves. See now, why would they wish to share something so utterly, divinely delicious and magical with you, when they could have it all for their own?'

So, Little Mouse Whiskey returned to Mother Sasli and asked, 'Mother Sasli, are you sure you don't wish to keep me from the cheese so you might eat it all yourself? If it is good cheese then we should surely share it.'

'Little Mouse Whiskey,' said Mother Sasli, 'You know I always share the food I find for us. No scrap or morsel is set before us that I do not divide fairly. When would I have given you reason to doubt me so?'

'I'm sorry, Mother Sasli – I do believe you. Truly, I do.'

And so Little Mouse Whiskey returned to the edge of the mouse-hole to sit downstream of the delicious aroma once more. And Iyagi the Kitchencat was there waiting for him.

'Mother Sasli always splits her food evenly with me, Mr Kitchencat,' said Little Mouse Whiskey. 'If she fancied the cheese, then this too she would share.'

'Oh, Little Mouse Whiskey,' said Iyagi the Kitchencat, secretly delighting in the naivety of his little mouse friend, 'Surely you are too smart to be fooled by such words. Of course she would tell you that – for nothing is greater of taste to a mouse than cheese. No doubt she shares mere crumbs and morsels to silence and fatten you while she keeps the cheese for herself.'

'That doesn't sound right, Mr Kitchencat.'

'Why not poke out your head and see for yourself?'

So Little Mouse Whiskey poked his head from the mouse-hole and saw the cheese, all bright and golden, sitting on a strange wooden block with spindly metal arms. No jaws awaited him; no stomping feet to crush his bones or poisons to tear at his innards.

'Do you see, little Mouse Whiskey,' said Iyagi the Kitchencat, alone on the wooden floor. 'See how the cheese waits for you, alone and in safety? Oh, I see many a mouse come by and take their fill of it. They smack their lips and hum-a-yum as they go, so they do.'

'Then why not fetch the cheese for me, Kitchencat, if no danger awaits me?'

'Me? But surely you know that no cat can touch cheese? The moment a poor, weak Kitchencat like me touches cheese of any kind, he shrivels and shrinks and wrinkles and wastes until he becomes a sultana with whiskers. Imagine! This, Little Mouse Whiskey, is the very worst fate for a cat. Surely, you do not wish me such a fate?'

'Oh, heavens no, Kitchencat! I do apologise, I do!'

So Little Mouse Whiskey scampered back to his mother and said:

'Mother Sasli, the cheese sits on a block of wood; a gift to us mice, for sure! There is no danger out there. Surely, I can take the cheese if I promise to bring it back to share?'

'Little Mouse Whiskey, you trouble me so,' said Mother Sasli, shaking her head and twitching her whiskers. 'See here, let me show you how safe that block of wood is.'

Now you and I surely know what that block of wood really was, but Little Mouse Whiskey had never seen or imagined anything so sinister in all his young weeks. Mother Sasli scurried into the shadows of the mouse-hole and pulled out a similar block of wood, roughly made but with the same spindly arms as the one in the kitchen that held the cheese. Little Mouse Whiskey noticed a strange rust-red stain deep in the grain. Mother Sasli laid down the wooden block and, with a mighty effort, pushed the metal arms till they ka-clicked flat to the wood.

'See, Little Mouse Whiskey,' said Mother Sasli, 'this is called a mouse trap – and it's the very same trap that caught dear Great Fathermouse Ernold.'

Suddenly, Mother Sasli threw a cherry stone at the trap, landing it just where the cheese would sit. Crack! The arms chopped shut and broke that cherry stone asunder! Quite overcome with fright, Little Mouse Whiskey leapt behind a gas pipe. His little black eyes popped wide and terrified, his nose a-twitching as any mouse's surely would.

'Do you see now, Little Mouse Whiskey? You must never step on a trap or it will break your back!'

So Little Mouse Whiskey crept back to the mouse-hole, where Iyagi the Kitchencat still purred, his furry tail swishing lazily though sunlit motes of dust.

'My Kitchencat, you led me astray! That trap is certainly a danger to little mice like me! My mother showed me how traps works and she showed me the arm of my long lost Great Fathermouse.'

'Oh, Little Mouse Whiskey!' said Iyagi the Kitchencat. 'But surely you know the truth about your Great Fathermouse? About cheese? How a mouse might never need his arms? No?'

Little Mouse Whiskey said nothing, but his ears were pricked and his eyes bright.

'Your Great Fathermouse did indeed eat the cheese, and it's true that he lost his arms. But that is only because he grew wings, Little Mouse Whiskey: great, white wings with which to soar and glide.'

Little Mouse Whiskey wiggled his nose and moved out to the middle of the kitchen. The smell was stronger, more inviting. Iyagi the Kitchencat prowled low beside him.

'Yes, and you know what makes them grow wings? Cheese. It is a journey every young mouse must take; those brave enough to overcome their fears and eat the cheese will earn their wings and dance among the clouds. Those who are too cowardly will forever live in dark kitchen holes.'

Little Mouse Whiskey continued to scamper slowly across the kitchen floor, skipping over the floorboards.

'Surely you've seen them, if you've ever glanced up to the window? Those swift shapes in the sky? They were once mice – I fool you not! Don't you remember how free they looked? Didn't you ever wish to be so free?'

Little Mouse Whiskey walked right up to the cheese. How magical, the kitchencat's stories of stealthily beating mother Sasli to the cheese; growing his wings and taking his place up in the sky among his brethren and gaining wonderful, infinite freedom. What an adventure!

'You've made it to the cheese, Little Mouse Whiskey! I knew you would! You've earned it for your bravery. Tell the other sky flyers about me – tell them to visit poor old me, stuck down here in the kitchen forever!'

And Little Mouse Whiskey reached out for the cheese. And as he took it, the trap snapped shut on him and broke his back. Oh, how he squealed – the sound too terrible for words! He wiggled his toes and called out for help but no more could he do to end his troubles.

'Foolish little mouse!' laughed Iyagi the Kitchencat. 'Even after your mother showed you a trap, you were still too greedy and impatient to bear her heed!'

And Iyagi the Kitchencat lay down on the wooden floor, tucked his front paws under his chest and purred, watching the final, frantic little struggles of Little Mouse Whiskey.

Little Mouse Whiskey

The Pommasaurus Problem

There once was a time when a vast land of agriculture found itself broken beneath a formidable oppression. The land was used to its long history of prosperity and influence built on many centuries' trade of the beautiful golden apples that grew only on its rich, red soil. Other nations coveted the sweet fruit and bought the apples by the shipload, paying handsomely for the produce and always returning for more. The Land of the Golden Apples had stamped its position on the world map, its heart beating golden. But now it was in crisis.

For the apples that had raised their cities had proven unbearably attractive to a much larger consumer – one that did not care for trade or formality: the Pommasaurs.

The Pommasaurs were giant creatures: they stood taller than churches, their red-scaled skin striped with bright yellow; their bulbous bellies swinging with the pendulous gravity of tower bells; their pug snouts leading a trail of thorny spines all the way to the end of their heavy tails. They were born from the craters of the many bubbling, steaming volcanoes that scorched the land. Rising in the morning, they sleepily plodded their great weight in hazy meanders to the irresistible savour of the golden orchards. Towns, livestock and people were crushed underfoot as the great beasts were ignorant of the human population and haunted only by their desire for golden sustenance. Their snub noses twitched and wiggled as the scent of the orchards grew stronger, until they could graze in the afternoon sun and chew the trees clean. By twilight they returned to their volcanic homes, where they would rest underground and leave the nights peaceful in their slumber. Day by day, the devastation grew as towns were stamped to rubble, lives were swatted out and the harvest diminished as men feared the approach of the feeding Pommasaurus.

Due to their formidable size and fierce armoured scales, the Pommasaurs were fiendishly difficult to slay. Very few had been successfully hunted – and none without loss and injury to the hunters who tried to bring them down. So, the King of the Land of Golden Apples turned to the Society of Curiosity – the noble branch of thinking men and women – and ordered them to realise his drastic new plan, one that would bring an end to the dark and terrible age of the Pommasaurus.

By order of the King, the royal decree stated, *an initiative has been put to accord: volcanoes are no longer permitted to exist in this nation. The people of the Land of Golden Apples must work to remove these abominations that give birth to the dreaded Pommasaurs.*

And so, on the highest order, the King's chemists researched day and night, finally developing a viscous liquid that could be poured right into the mouths of the volcanoes. Upon contact with the molten interior, the liquid would rubberise and cool, killing the volcano and sealing the opening. The volcano would be reduced to a mere mountain. When the chemists announced their successful formula, the nation cheered and readied itself for deployment. The King, overcome with glee, called the solution 'Rooberjuice'.

Manufacturers from every corner of the land worked together tirelessly to process the solution, storing it away in many great vats and drums that soon lined the fields, far from the ambling paths of the Pommasaurs. The newspapers and journals ran daily stories hailing the great efforts to fight against the hated giants that climbed from the earth every morning; the people were united by this one great effort to change things for the better. There was hope at last!

In a bid to avoid vengeful counterattacks from an angered army of Pommasaurs, each and every volcano in the land had to be filled in one swift, manic evening. Not a single Pommasaur could be allowed to walk the land again.

The wise engineers designed great vehicles that could pump whole vats of Rooberjuice into the cavernous mouths of the volcanoes; great, hulking, machines with black, clawed tyres and growling engines lined the edges of the Rooberjuice fields, ready to be fired up and sent forth.

When the sun set on the Pommasaurs' final day of freedom, the frenzied country steadied itself. The Pommasaurs yawned their great mouths, indifferent to the mood of the nation, and lumbered back to the magma, their hearts content and their bellies filled with apples. As the last Pommasaur retreated into the last volcano, a thousand lights shone over the fields as the vehicles burst into life. The Land of the Golden Apples held its breath.

The roads blistered under the weight of the vehicles as they raced to fulfil their duty. The people waited in their battered homes, arms locked in trepidation. From their darkened windows, they watched the lights of the tractors move across the land like stars swept to black holes.

And when the sun rose, every volcano was filled. There was quiet. The dawn paled to mid-morning and not a rumble or a stomp was heard. In the warmth of the afternoon, the land relaxed, tense and aching chests deflating in sweet relief. Horizon to horizon, the world stood joined in celebration at the marvel of how small people had overcome great tribulation. For one glorious day there, was hope.

The next day, the country rose late from their post-jubilation, intoxicated slumber. Those in the capital stretched wide, looked out to the landscape and saw... a volcano. A bubbling, smoking mound belching ash before a lazy sun. A new volcano. And, from the crater, a line of hot, steaming magma footprints. The footprints continued all the way across the Royal Park, leading right up to a very happy-looking Pommasaur, who was busy munching on the King's personal golden orchard.

It was a disaster. The people in the Land of the Golden Apples had never been so disappointed.

The King, with righteous bile, launched his whole army upon the invading Pommasaur but, in its typical indifference, it shrugged them off as though they were no more than wasps. The King had one furious question on his mind: Who had dared build this new volcano? Who would wish to bring such a foul tiding upon his Golden Lands?

Men, women and all the people of the nation looked to each other with confusion. Why would any of them want for this? After all the effort to end the horror – why?

Bewilderment turned to speculation; speculation became suspicion. What about those foreign types that lived among the national, born of another land and perhaps not sharing in the values of the great golden nation. What of them? Surely they would be the first to build a volcano that would hatch new Pommasaurs and bring the land to its knees?

The foreigners protested of course: they wished no harm, they said. They had no means to construct a volcano! They hated the Pommasaurs, so they said! But the people born of the land were furious and sought the gratification of justice. So all the King's men rounded up 'those of tainted culture', arresting them, putting them on trial and sentencing them to immediate death for their treasonous acts. Now, the land was safe.

With the world free of further ill-wishery, they put the Rooberjuice back into action and destroyed the new rogue volcano, just as they had before. Peace stilled the chaos once more.

But two mornings later, three new volcanoes had erupted out of the crust, birthing more wandering Pommasaurs. Oh how the foreign folk must be glaring up at them through the soil of their graves. Who could be conniving enough to build volcanoes now? To the King, it was obvious.

'I have seen the schemers and the unpatriotic among you,' said the King. 'Those of you who march our streets and protest our ways of government. Yes, these anarchy-seekers who wish to change our beloved society would be happy to raise these volcanoes, unleashing the creatures beneath and spoiling these cherished lands.'

Of course! How clear it all was! What better way to topple a despised sovereignty than to unleash beasts to consume its most precious produce? So, in fear for their way of life, the people felt a malice ignite within them against the newly suspected anarchists. The politically disgruntled were sought out and dragged before judge and jury. And, in the haste to end the nightmare, the revolutionaries too were silenced at the blade of the executioner.

Once again, the people brought down the belching volcanoes with Rooberjuice, wiping sweat from their brows and backs for the third time. This time, however, the celebrations were suspended in mute anxiety as the folk waited, worried.

'The Nation's Breath', as the journals had dubbed it, was held in wait for the tectonic shiver that would signal another failure. One, two, and then three days passed without a tremor; not a soul dared move; the grass resisted the sway of the wind; the birds held back their chorus. But, on the fourth day, the air was once again choked black with ash as the land broke tall with steaming peaks and a thousand sighs released a hurricane's worth of disappointment.

Who? Who could be responsible? What wretched, villainous devil could continue to be so xenomasochistic? And why?

It was then, when the mood of the nation had swung down to its lowest ebb, that the Society of Curiosity stepped forward. They had been watching the efforts to curb the destruction being wrought by the Pommasaurs and the pointed fingers of blame that came in their wake. Questioning whether these volcanoes could really be the work of man, the Society suggested gently that to apportion blame among the people who made up this great golden land was foolish and divisive. The volcanoes may well be resurrecting for different reasons than subterfuge, they suggested.

And so the King executed each and every member of the Society of Curiosity, declaring their deflective behaviour to be far too suspicious.

And when the Pommasaurs still came, the King and his people were enveloped in a paranoia so fervent that it burned their minds to a thick fog and boiled their blood to a rush of acid.

They killed the women, fearing they were lashing out at the society that raised men on higher pedestals. But still the volcanoes rose.

They killed the poor, believing them to be resentful of the wealth that higher society had plucked from the Golden Apple trade. But still the volcanoes rose.

They killed the media, suspecting they had created the volcanoes as a way to fill their journals; the government and sub-monarchy for using the volcanoes as a means to coup; those who were allergic to apples; those who loved apples too much; the cryptozoologists; the volcanologists... they executed them all.

But still the volcanoes rose.

And after weeks and months of bloodshed and failure, the only people left living in all the land were the King and his premier, personal army. The King, sitting hunched on his fists, knew full well that it was not he who continued to build the volcanoes that hatched the Pommasaurs, so the only culprit must be one of his men. Of course, he cried. It all finally made sense, for they were the only ones with the cunning, training and power to accomplish such acts. They were the ones he'd least expect: it had been the perfect crime. But no more! The King was not a forgiving man: he promptly ordered his armies to fill the remaining volcanoes and then marched them – one, two, one, two – over a cliff.

Finally, the King was alone. The world was silent, but for his breath and the call of songbirds the leaves of the apple trees. He walked, fully robed in his royal colours, shining among the Golden Apples and glorious in the knowledge that he could rebuild his Kingdom and claim the riches for himself. No conspiring underlings, no covetous citizens and most importantly – no Pommasaurs! He plucked a Golden Apple from the nearest tree and feasted on it in victory, the sweet cider glistening stickily in his beard.

But the moment soured. Quietly, the soil began to unsettle. Then it grew hot – so hot his toes began to burn and his legs were drenched in sweat. Before his small eyes, the volcanoes rose around him, towering and spilling forth copious magma. They grew from the inside out, until they burst open, hot and deafening. The Golden Apple dropped from the King's hands and he stumbled backwards, his jaw gaping limply from his skull. Now the true architects were revealed. Not the work of human labour, vengeance, anger or uprising, these vengeful volcanoes, but the simple nature of the beast. They rose at the will of the Pommasaurs; it was their way: they pushed and clawed their way through the earth until the magma broke free and hissed in the cool morning air.

The King fell to his behind and watched as the Pommasaurs clambered from their underground chambers and drew greedily upon his golden fruit. They chomped at the trees, and licked their scaled lips, their tails swaying contentedly. Each footstep shook the ground and the Golden Apples jangled in the trees like festive bells. He had no people to fight for him: no army, subjects or well-wishers. He was alone with only Pommasaurs and fast-diminishing acres of the sweet Golden Apples for company. Delicious and beautiful they were, but no defence or company. So, running on tired, fattened legs, the King finally retreated from his own land and set sail for a neighbouring nation to live his remaining days in bored aristocracy. He slipped aboard a boat at the empty docks and sailed it out across the ocean. But without a crew or a captain, he soon became disorientated and lost in the vastness of the waters, never to see land again.

And so the great Pommasaurs claimed a nation unto their own. For hundreds of years they reigned peacefully among the Golden Orchards, living long, lazy lives. And no one saw how the dark volcanic soil became enriched with Pommasaurus manure, how the young saplings spread and flourished and how tall, thick and beautiful the multitudes of Golden Apple trees grew.

The Le Jambon Effect

The Le Jambon Effect

Everyone remembers where they were in the day of the first headsplosion. Not least those in the front row of Elegarte Theatre, when the brains of the world's finest thespian, Bruce le Jambon, burst his skull to shards and splattered their haughty faces. His eyeballs were never found. Some said they were stolen as mementoes of that day, others hinted that they had been eaten by hungry theatre rats.

At any rate, Bruce le Jambon had made an indelible mark in history, if not for any of the reasons he'd hoped. A statue had been commissioned to sit in the foyer of Elegarte Theatre in his honour, although, due to disagreements over whether its head should be complete or exploded, it was never built.

The painful truth, however, was that even le Jambon's dramatic death did not mark him out as exceptional. Within the week, two more cases had been reported. By the month's end, it was declared an epidemic. Officially, they called it the le Jambon effect. There was little idea whether it was caused by disease, mutation or attack; they only agreed that they hated the distasteful 'headsplosion' colloquialism that had quickly become popular.

Of course, the order to find a cure came from Queen Conniece herself. The gravity cut across her forehead, throwing strange shadows over her eyes in the twilight as she looked out over her kingdom: a disarray of homes and buildings pocked with warm-lit windows. Each building housed perhaps a handful of her people, all terrified of the pox that might sneak upon them like a stranger in the night. She considered herself a good queen, a devoted matriarch, and she would certainly not be defeated by such vulgar, despicable nonsense.

So, she did what anyone would do in such times of need – she turned to the Thinquers. The House of Thinque was an elite body of people distinguished by their acute study of the world around them. The Thinquers wrote heavy, unreadable tomes on the ways of the world and on vague ideas that had brewed among them in the small hours. The House had grown over the centuries from a small clique of enlightened friends that met in a pub corner on drunken Sunday afternoons to an intellectual powerhouse. It was now far beyond doubt that the Thinquers, more than anyone else, added a strong backbone to the vast body of human ideas.

Queen Conniece, by emissary, demanded that they arrest the spread of the dreadful condition and, under the stewardship of their head, Professor Peeples, they immediately set to task. They started by claiming the right to every le Jambonned body in the land for study.

Now, Professor Peeples was a woman of strict standard. Though her size was petite for a woman, her strength of character amplified her stature so that she seemed to cast a shadow over every corner of the House of Thinque. Her pace was marked by the light, rhythmic jingle from her silver anklets, a sound that the Thinquers grew to find both haunting and invigorating. She ensured that every cadaver was squeezed, so to speak, of every last drop of evidence that could lay a trail to the root of the problem. The Thinquers produced reams of carefully written documentation in tiny, improbably curly scrawl on pale parchment that detailed every circumstance, blemish and irregularity on the unfortunates. Through long days and nights, they inked, re-inked and studied their notes, even muralling great plots across the open, white walls of the House of Thinque. And, before long, Professor Peeples stood before an anticipating public to declare their first discovery of interest: that the le Jambon effect was always preceded by a tickling sensation of the hand and a slight dizziness!

Professor Peeples expected the public to delight in this premier breakthrough. Instead, they saw every tickle and tingle as forewarning of impending cranial explosion and worked themselves into a dizziness of paranoia that rushed over the land like a storm.

The reaction from the Palais was far from temperate. The Queen smouldered, her posterior flung back into her throne, her heels drumming against the red carpet, her fingers working furiously into her clenched temples. Working her people into chaos was absolutely not the job of the Thinquers and her remonstration was severe. After a personal and furious denunciation, dictated enthusiastically by a young emissary, she forbade the Thinquers from any further public declaration, insisting that all their research must pass through the Palais. She assigned her well-seasoned mediator, Lord Deparler, to transmit information from the House of Thinque to the Palais. All further breakthroughs that resulted from their research were to be communicated directly to Deparler. He smiled a greeting at the Thinquers from over his silver-tipped cane, his overworked face sagging from his many years of public speaking.

Cowed by this misappropriation of their research, the Thinquers returned to work with heavy hearts. They knew that they would struggle to ever find a cure for the le Jambon effect, as the headsplosions came so suddenly from the preceding symptoms, but perhaps they could concoct a prevention. If they could protect everyone in advance, why, they wouldn't have to worry about le Jambon Effect at all!

As the headless, stinking bodies continued to pile up in the once-beautiful courtyard of the House of Thinque, Peeples's people worked the skin from their fingers and the hair from their heads in search of an answer. They poked and pickled, burned and boiled, distilled and desiccated, lifting every technique from the ever-expanding Book of Thinque until they were confident to discuss their findings with Lord Deparler.

Lord Deparler was a wealthy man – a fact evidenced by a belly straining from a lifetime of fine dining. He refused, however, to elevate himself above the public – it was his job to communicate the word from on high down to the common folk, so he deemed it most important that he be seen as part of the community. Thus, wherever possible, he walked from place to place. Certainly, he was hemmed into fine suits and topped with a jaunty, gold-brimmed hat, but he marched the same streets as everybody else and people were well used to his presence among them. Unfortunately, this tended to make him quite late for all his meetings.

When he finally arrived at the House of Thinque, his cane tock-tocking along the flagstone courtyard, Professor Peeples was tense from the long anticipation. She showed him to the dining room, which was littered with the fewest corpses in the house. He sat dangerously close to the edge of his chair, his weight held forward over his knees, his gaze flickering around the room, his fitted jacket clinging uncomfortably to his plumpness. He preferred to sit forward as he imagined he looked engaged and excited, but Professor Peeples found his posture intimidating; her skin prickled in his presence, despite her confidence in the Thinquers' study.

'This is the story so far,' Peeples told him. 'The one thing all the unfortunates share is a strange chemical in their blood we've called Jamboline. It is almost certain that someone who suffers a headsplosion – I should say, someone who displays this particularly unpleasant symptom – suffers due to an infection of this chemical.'

'Mmm, mmm – that is a jolly good find!' said Deparler. 'But what can you people do about it, eh?'

'Well, we believe we've managed to create a counter-chemical – an 'Evil Twin' of Jamboline, if you will – that cripples it in the blood. We suspect that if we give someone the Evil Twin they will be protected from the le Jambon effect.'

'Why, that's marvellous!' Deparler chuckled back into his chair. 'We're bloody saved!'

'But wait!' said Peeples. Her eyes locked keenly with his, for this was important. 'These are early days. We cannot throw the Evil Twin out to the people, no matter how scared they are. Oh, it certainly works here in the House but what if we find out it can make your toes rot to ash or force your teeth to grow until they push your jaw from your skull? We need volunteers. We need testing. We need time. But, I assure you, we have great hopes that this is the breakthrough we've been waiting for.'

Lord Deparler sank a little in his chair but caught himself before his disappointment became too obvious. Instead, he shook Professor Peeples's hand, wished her good luck and departed for the Queen's attention.

For Lord Deparler, this latest revelation was troubling. He did not like Professor Peeple's speculative talk of 'early days' and 'testing' and 'hope'. How disenchanting! On the twisting walk over the cobbled streets to the Palais, the Lord rolled the Professor's non-committal information silently over his tongue. He wondered how to stand before Queen Conniece and frame the development as something meaningful. Did the Queen and her people really want to hear news of yet more waiting? This news was stony grey in a world that desperately yearned for colour.

So, bowing before Queen Conniece, the Lord took a gamble. He told her that the Thinquers had found a cure. Oh, how the Queen rose from her seat – the weight of her worries lifting so rapidly that she appeared, for a moment, to be floating on air. Energised by Deparler's good news, she gambolled through the Palais with such merriment that the long train of her royal frock barely touched the ground behind her. Her aides and guards scampered and chased behind her, crashing into furniture as they tried to keep up with her flight. Queen Conniece burst into the open air of the royal balcony overlooking the main public square. With a barely-suppressed air of victory and a raised fist, she gave the good tidings to a cheering citizenry. The darkness was lifting.

But in a sea of public adulation, the House of Thinque was an island of panic. How on Earth could their message have unravelled so horribly? The gin decanters ran dry as the Thinquers buried themselves under the momentary comfort of intoxication. They were nowhere near ready to present the Evil Twin to the world.

Professor Peeples banged on the gates of the Palais, demanding to see Lord Deparler. But a guard told her, over his nose, that Deparler had given her all the presence she required and that she would do well to start prepare the Evil Twin for the masses. Incensed, Peeples refused and locked down the doors of the House. She told the Palais that her Thinquers would follow the testing schedule as planned. She would not release the Evil Twin until it was ready, and that was that.

Lit umber by a dusky sun, Queen Conniece sat upon her throne, her face scrunched and her body tense. Her fingers rattled on the arm of her throne. How could the Thinquers withhold the solution to mankind's greatest woe? How could she help her people if the only ones with the key of salvation had locked themselves away? She called upon Deparler, who had been curiously inconspicuous of late.

'Perhaps it is a matter of gold,' he posited. 'The House of Thinque is a proud institution and there is a chance their arrogance stems from feeling undervalued?'

Of course, Deparler had never truly considered this to be a matter of money. He was a proud man and was hardly ready to renege on his earlier embellishments, so he thought a little further moulding of the truth might mend matters. Maybe, just maybe, the Thinquers could be coerced into accelerating their studies with a little more weight in their pockets. But he would never test that idea, as his theories served only to outrage the Queen, who now saw the Thinquers as villains, prepared to hold the sick and fearful to ransom.

In the meantime, the people continued to live in paralysing fear of the le Jambon effect. They spent their days all a-quiver, knowing that, at any moment, the head of their nearest and dearest could burst into a sticky mess. Many had taken to tattooing their names onto their bodies in case they were ever found alone and headless.

Drawn to impatience and unable to admit his part in the debacle, Lord Deparler felt he had no choice but to spur the House of Thinque forward through public disgrace. He released word that the Thinquers were holding back due to their greed. He was so caught up in his own desperate truth-spinning that he'd almost started to believe the twists in his tale. The people were understandably furious. They rioted at the gates of the House of Thinque, shaking the iron frames on their hinges and cursing out the Thinquers inside. If language really could turn the air blue, then the House of Thinque would long be lost in a thick soup of cobalt fog. Women and men marched angry circles around the once-esteemed establishment, chanting and yelling, waving banners and stomping out tribal rhythms. So lengthy were the protestations that three rioters suffered headsplosions, soiling the mob and forcing them all home to bathe.

As the crisis grew, rogue schools of self-styled academics began to emulate Professor Peeples's faltering House of Thinque. The idea went that, if they worked long and hard enough, they too could find a cure of sorts and put an end to the headsplosive horror. Unfortunately, these dubious masters of the intellectual revolution had never dabbled in relevant matters before and, though they were experts in their individual teachings, they were quite unprepared to take on the le Jambon effect. Nonetheless, with their heads firmly to the chalkboard and brimming over with only the best of intentions, the Strong Skulls – a group of former army officers – were the first to present their solution: Hazel Helmets. You see, it had long been believed (for reasons buried in antiquity) that hazel had healing properties. So, the Strong Skulls reasoned that if they carved the wood of the hazel tree into a helmet that it would surely protect the head from the outside-in.

The public went crazy for the helmets, snapping them up as fast as the hazel trees could be chopped down. Even Queen Conniece wore a special crown inset, fashioned with a Hazel Helmet core. The Thinquers spoke out against the helmets, declaring them to be a ridiculous insanity, but they were shouted away by the helmeted crowds who mocked them for having produced precisely nothing to help them. The people thought them jealous of the Strong Skulls. The Queen, though personally uncertain of the Hazel Helmets, thought them better than nothing and continued to wear hers. Behind the closed doors of the House of Thinque, Professor Peeples gathered the Thinquers and reminded them that, the sooner they could produce a real solution, the sooner people would turn their faces away from the desperate solutions of fringe groups.

Naturally, the helmets did not work. The le Jambon effect continued to wreak its nastiness and, in one memorable case, a judge's head exploded inside her helmet in such a manner as to leave her face completely intact and impassive, hanging loosely at the opening of her helmet with the rest of her broken head sloshing behind. Four witnesses took to the stand in court that day before anyone realised she had died.

Despite the helmets' disappointing results, the Strong Skulls, in their arrogance, insisted on their efficacy. And the people clung to that optimism as they might to driftwood over a waterfall. Still, Professor Peeples kept the House of Thinque locked down, working on an Evil Twin that they could scatter to the masses without fear of disaster.

From the marketplace, a scrawny pedlar named Oppo had kept his eyes and ears keen. He saw how the public clamoured for answers and how they would grasp and claw at anything put before them. After the Hazel Helmets, all manner of silly solutions had appeared – from shoes to cakes to dances. From beneath his dirty cloak, he saw an opening for some peddling that would fill the cracks made by fear. If the people wanted hope, then hope is what he would sell them – no more, no less. By the moon he stole, over tracks and dales to farmlands. With his spindly arms, he drew a blade as long as his arm and cut the head from the largest ox in the field with one fierce swing. Tucking the horns under his arm, he brought the head to his home and, by candlelight, pounded and ground it until it was nowt but a fine paste, fit for bottling. By the dawn, he had filled and labelled over one hundred jars with 'Oppo's Oxhead Paste'.

As custom decreed, he took the paste to the Palais, presenting a jar from bended knee.

'Grown from the earth, 'tis!' said Oppo, his head bowed. 'Will make your head as strong as an ox, it will.'

Now, Oppo was poor and weasley, but he was no fool. He feared the turn of the mob at the inevitable failure of his paste, so he threw in a condition:

'Now, you be sure to scrub that paste deep into your temples at the exact stroke o' midnight. No sooner, no later, mind, or it won't do nothin' for you, it won't.'

Deparler was given custody of the jar of Oxhead Paste and he chose to pass it to the Thinquers for their appraisal, hoping to have found a breakthrough at long last. Intrigued, the Thinquers examined the paste with their tools and chemicals, and under their magnificent bulbous lenses. They declared, with regret, that the paste was no more than beef-swill – certainly no solution to the le Jambon effect, but perhaps fit for a fine broth, when mixed with a little coriander. They dismissed Lord Deparler swiftly so that they could continue to focus on a real resolution.

Deparler was most dismayed. He had expected to return to the Queen with the glorious news of a headsplosion-free future, but instead he had a jar of cow juice. As the rain hit his umbrella as he hurried up the path to the Palais, he reasoned that another little tweak of the truth could nicely bridge the time until the Thinquers completed their task.

'What I hold before me, is Oppo's Oxhead Paste,' he said, before the Queen. 'The Thinquers could nary make head or tails of it, but they are far too busy on the Evil Twin. Its inventor is extremely confident, though, I must say.'

'Fine, Deparler,' said the Queen, keeping her head firmly rested on the wing of her throne. 'Distribute it to the people as you wish. Let them try it for themselves.'

Professor Peeples was most annoyed, but even she understood the tension of an anxious nation. Just the previous day an elderly lady had headsploded into a bowl of cake batter. Unfortunately, her body had fallen out of sight and into the larder. Her husband, upon finding the unmade batter, continued to fashion it into their granddaughter's birthday cake as planned. Only after it had been consumed by fifteen excited toddlers had the terrible truth come to light. Nobody wished to hear more stories like that.

But of course, Oppo's Oxhead Paste had no effect on le Jambon, though the mood of the people had certainly lifted. They credited the continued presence of headsplosions to the difficulty of applying the paste at the exact moment of midnight and not on the paste itself. If anyone was affected by the le Jambon effect, it was easier to digest if it was their own fault for not using the paste properly. Far more satisfying to fault the individual than an unexplained mysterious affliction.

As time strode on, the likes of the Strong Skulls and Oppo grew richer and the House of Thinque further lost the affection of the public. The red brick of the House was dashed with eggshell, dried in yellow yolk and rotting red streaks of old tomatoes.

Finally though, after all the toil, the Thinquers were satisfied that they had created an Evil Twin solution strong enough to prevent the le Jambon effect and safe enough for those that took it. Professor Peeples, who had grown stiff and flushed, finally allowed herself to exhale. She sat in her narrow window-side armchair with her hands hanging loosely over its arms and a small glass of whiskey held from her fingertips. The ice shrank away as she allowed herself to drift into the quiet relief of unfocused thoughtlessness.

They called on Lord Deparler to present their solution for the Queen. They let him thumb through their many stacks of papers and drawings. They showed him their experiments, their volunteers – none of those who had imbibed the Evil Twin had fallen victim to the le Jambon effect, while those who had taken a fake Evil Twin had headsploded as frequently as any other. They walked him through the story of the Evil Twin's inception, speaking keenly as if presenting their own child. Lord Deparler had to summon several aides just to carry the documents up to the Palais.

And Queen Conniece waved the Evil Twin by with a bored flick of her bejewelled hand, directing it to the neglected accumulation of hokum pocum that grew dusty in the west courtyard. She had lost all hope in supposed cures.

Instead of carrying a Palais seal of approval, the Thinquers were expected to trade their own solution like any other peddler. The Evil Twin found itself stalled at market between the Hazel Helmets and Oppo's Oxhead Paste with nothing to distinguish itself as the product of long, intellectual labour.

But the people who passed their stall stopped only to spit and gesture aggressively in their direction. The Thinquers had lost their lustre. They had locked themselves away while the people were begging for their aid and only now – when cures were a thriving, booming business – had they reappeared with their wares. Furthermore, they came without the back story of the Strong Skulls or the charm of Oppo. They spoke in a weird, clinical tongue that the people distrusted. And ultimately, their Evil Twin was bitterly foul to the taste. Why should they choose this expensive, foul chemical solution when they could have the natural purity of the Oxhead Paste or the tangible security of the Hazel Helmet? And everyone had heard the Palais gossip: that Queen Conniece wore a crown of Hazel and had her courtiers timed her Oxhead pasting to the exactness of midnight with diamond-cut clocks. The Queen's head remained as intact and robust on her body as it was upon their coins. What greater endorsement than that?

And so the Evil Twin grew dusty and old at market. Professor Peeples looked at the Thinquers and saw disappointed faces; she looked out to the world and saw exploded heads. She was shaken and troubled. She stood before the people with clenched fists to her bosom:

'I implore you, you must see sense! The time long spent on the Evil Twin was for you! We were locked away to focus on getting it right – all for you!'

But it was too late. The trust in the Thinquers had long since passed and the public turned on Peeples for insisting she knew best. They could stand no more of her arrogance and, as tradition dictated, they chased her and her Thinquers out of the land with flaming pitchforks. They chased them across fields, over walls, through forests and over rivers. And, when their pitchforks had burned to a few melted prongs, they knew that the Thinquers would never return. So they shook their fists one last time at the fleeing dots on the horizon and headed home.

The Thinquers reached the coast, boarded an old ferry and left for lands across the water. Some of the Thinquers patted each other heartily and spoke of how they were glad to be rid of such senseless people. But Professor Peeples watched the old land grow small on the water and saw only senselessly, unnecessarily exploded heads. And the dry wind whipped the tears across her cheeks.

Back at home, the people continued to wear their Hazel Helmets. Since everybody wore them, people started decorating them in paint and ornaments and wore them proudly, like a coat of arms. They still applied their paste at every stroke of midnight, a tradition that lasted long after old Oppo's own head popped wet and sticky splatters over his mansion's mink carpets. They still mocked those foolish enough to have mistimed their application. They smiled with self-satisfaction as those around them lost their heads, showing themselves to be lesser beings than the survivors. And the cities built giant, flowering, abstract monuments from the discarded Hazel Helmets stained with blood, brain and bull paste. The monuments grew taller and more expansive, casting great shadows over the people who walked beneath them, waiting for the moment to take them.

Sewing Box, Mallet & Carving Knife

In a little village you probably haven't heard of, a boy named Paphil and a girl named Aimemes grew up together in little brick cottages at opposite ends of a community pasture. They had both tended to the cattle for as long as they could walk, so their entire childhood had been spent in each other's company. In the ascent of their maturity and the storm of their bodily changes, they found their insides were tugged into blossoming realisations about their very natures. Paphil realised that he loved Aimemes more than anything or anyone he'd ever known in all the small world he lived in. Aimemes, however, realised that she only bore goosebumps of desire and heartache for other women.

One luminous evening in early summer, as Paphil and Aimemes were attempting to coax a cow back to her shed by the tried-and-tested method of poking its rump with sticks, Paphil fell to his dusty knees before Aimemes with his bottom lip gripped firmly between his teeth.

'Oh, Aimemes,' he said between tiny gasps. 'You are the stirrup to my horse, the hoe to my earth, the ladybird to my aphid-infested tomato plant. Please say I can be yours and let us be more than just a boy and a girl poking a cow.'

'Oh, dearest, sweet Paphil,' she said, taking his cow-poking hand in hers. 'You are the loveliest boy I have ever known. But my heart opens only for a lady's love.'

And they finished herding the stubborn cow in silence, but for the prodding thuds of sticks on beef.

Paphil, disappointed but determined, returned home and snuck into his mother's dresser. Sitting before her mirror, he tied his mop of blonde hair into two high pigtails. Then, he plucked at her powders, brushes and pencils, colouring and blushing his face into a mimicry of the ladies he'd seen sipping tea on spindly chairs down by the river's edge. As for his wispy, ambitious beard hairs: he pulled them out one by one, until he was as smooth as a hard-boiled egg.

In the morning times, as the birds' chorus quelled and the sunlight caught the eastern hedgerow, Paphil returned to the cattle shed to release the cows to graze. He found Aimemes already inside, untying the gates and winding the loose rope to a loop along her forearm.

'Look Aimemes,' he said, arms wide and smiling. 'I look like a girl – a lady! Surely you can consider me now!'

'Oh Paphil,' Aimemes sighed. 'Your gesture: it's more flattering than the way these cow-tending dungarees of mine flatter my backside. You see in my smile my love for you; my lips turn up and my heart is forced to take a moment's pause in sheer wonder and appreciation. But under that make-up, dear Paphil, you are still a boy and I do not turn for boys.'

Paphil nodded and they worked the rest of the day without passing mention of the unrequited moments of the morning. But he saw how the bull in the neighbouring field stood at the barbed wire divide and eyed the cows with an undisguised longing, digging his hoofs into the grass and huffing out sprays of spittle. Paphil glanced from the horns of the bulls to the bulging swinging udders of the cows.

That night, he stole down to the kitchen, across the cold, tiled floor to the old oak drawers. In the blue of midnight, he took the cook's best carving knife and cut two deep slits over his chest. Then, he took the heavy milk can from the larder and carefully tipped the spout to the fresh slits, first the left and then the right. His pectorals filled with the cool milk till they bulged heavily like hanging pink pears. He stitched the slits up and returned to bed, satisfied with his efforts.

The next morning, he made sure to remake his face as before and wear his tightest cloth shirt to emphasise and support his milky bosom. When he met Aimemes at pasture, he stood tall and thrust his chest forward, crying:

'See how I am womanly, Aimemes! I bear the ample curves of a lady to match my fair-painted face! Surely now you can love me as your own?'

He batted his long-blackened eyelashes for her, for emphasis. But Aimemes sighed with a soft tilt of her head. Her smile did not shine as it had the previous morning, but hung limp and weak on her face.

'Paphil – you may bear the chest of a woman, and a very fine chest, indeed, but you are still a boy. No, I must say you are a man, to be true. And though you may be as wonderful and sweet a man for which one could ever wish, I bear no fibres in my being that can love a man – even if he does have exceptional breasts.'

And Paphil was disheartened but polite. He nodded again and completed the day's work with her. Aimemes painted the silence with all manner of chitter-chatter about the quick change of the seasons and her utter inability to make a decent pie. But his thoughts were snagged on how to unlock her devotion and her words were lost in the air between them.

Before retiring to bed that night, he crept a patter through the house, stealing items from various rooms: the carving knife from the chef, the sewing kit from his father and a heavy mallet from his mother.

He lay in bed, naked in cool half-moon light, curling and relaxing his toes in rhythm with heavy breaths. He brought the vision of Aimemes into his head and fixed it behind his eyes. He saw her in the height of summer, out in the field, the afternoon sun catching her contours in gold, her lightly heat-blushed cheeks, her long brown neck; the tightening of her back, exposed beneath her high-tied shirt as it flowed into the curves of her behind...

He held his erection in one hand and, with a fierce swish, cut it clean off with the carving knife.

'Away from me, you foul appendage!' he whispered.

He took the severed end of his erection and tied it up tight, to keep its firm turgidity, like how his father used to make balloons from sheep's bladders. Then, holding the bleeding stump to his pelvis, he hammered the erection into himself, bringing the mallet down hard again and again and again, till only the ties showed. The erection forced a hollow where his penis had once been. He pulled the penis from the hollow, pinched the outer skin to a pleat and sewed himself as pretty a pair of labia as he could. He had sewed as long as his clothes had worn, and so he confidently worked his groin to beauty.

When Aimemes arrived at the pasture the next morn, clumsily squashing her boots through the rain-soaked, hoof-trodden mud, Paphil was already waiting for her. He was leaning casually against a cow, one foot crossed before the other. He had cut his work trousers to tiny shorts, his skin plucked smooth, he faced powdered with his mother's make-up and his shirt tied to cradle his breasts.

'Paphil, what are you doing so early?' she asked him.

'I am all-woman now,' he replied. 'For you!'

'Paphil, you cannot be all woman, for you are a man. Just as this cow will never be a midnight burlesque performer, so you can never be a woman for me!'

Paphil stumbled slightly, pulling away from the cow, who showed no signs of burlesque-related heartbreak as she nonchalantly ruminated cud back into her mouth.

'No, Aimemes – you must see what I've done!' Paphil tugged down his shorts to reveal his new groin, neatly sewn to a divide and capped in a curly, topiary heart.

'Oh, Paphil...'

'You see, we can be together, you and I!'

'Oh, Paphil, I cannot say how flattered I am that you'd sculpt a vulva from your own flesh for me. That you'd move through the motions you think all women must and shape your body to the way you think a female must be. But you are not a woman, you are a man.'

'No, see – I am a woman. I can be a woman!' Paphil ripped the clothes from his body and stood naked before Aimemes, trying to balance in an elegant pose, all polished limbs and bosominess. He pouted his lips and tilted his hips.

'Close your eyes, Paphil,' Aimemes said quietly.

He closed his eyes and she took his shoulders in her hands.

'Your body is changed. You look like a woman to me, and I know women. But forget your flesh, dear Paphil, for I do not speak of your body when I call you a man. Look inside yourself. How do you see yourself – as man or woman? Who is Paphil, truly?'

Paphil let a deep breath flow through his lips slowly.

'Yes, inside I am a man, but –'

'Shhh,' said Aimemes. 'You are a man, as you have always been and so you should be. You are fooling only yourself. You are the wonderful Paphil, whom I have always loved and so you should remain. Be true to me and be true to yourself.'

A pause. A sigh.

'Oh, Aimemes, you're right,' said Paphil. 'I'm no woman, no girl or lady. You and I can never be, for you will never want me and how could I ever be with someone who cannot love me back?'

They embraced, Paphil's breasts pulling the old dirt from Aimemes's overalls.

'Perhaps you can teach me to be a woman,' Paphil whispered over her shoulder. 'I don't know if I can undo what I have done.'

'There is no formbook to being a woman,' she said, taking his hand. 'Just be beautiful you.'

He smiled.

'But maybe we can try to get yourself back to the way you were, if you'll let me help,' she added.

They unwound their embrace and let their handhold linger for a few moments. Then they collected themselves and set to a hard day's work and by that summery afternoon, the air had grown thick with the bonds of true friendship and the stench of souring milk.

Vestradamus

That old and famous seer you know did also have a cousin,
And people came to hear him speak, a-gath'ring in their dozens,
But poor old Vestradamus, he attracted only mockers,
'Your sooths are stinking bunk!' they cried, 'Absurd, outlandish whoppers!'

He pointed his keen gaze towards the distant next millennium,
He saw men build giant atoms, like the so-called ununquadium;
They scoffed his sight of spaceships and of cars without a horse,
A man stood on the moon, well that was farcical of course.

Nostradamus saw burned cities, and his list'ners cowed, afraid,
He chilled imaginations with disaster-strewn parades,
The world banded together, in old Vestra's precognitions,
By tiny, bright devices – would mere men become magicians?

Of how we'd rule the earth, and sea, and skies and outer space,
The people branded blasphemous – the realm of God replaced,
But tales of war and Kings, and near impending tragedy,
Drove multitudes to listen to great Nostra's rhapsody.

So Vestra saved his wondrous sights, and focused on the chills:
God toppled by philosophy, and women on the pill,
City-crushing weapons; itchy fingers on the trigger,
'Come now,' cried the scorning crowd, 'Your lies can't get much bigger!'

So Vestradamus died in shame, his legend too was dead,
His body decomposed, around the world his atoms spread,
And now they sit in pills and oil, in plastics, bombs and phones,
You might even be reading from a page made from his bones.

Passage

Then

the world

grew up when

science unfurled

and then disabled

the people's beliefs in

their old wives' tales and fables.

But myths only sink to the skin

while the act of believing holds deep

inside the nature of being human.

So, into your enlightened minds thoughts creep

of ways to have faith, so that you can

feel you control more than a mote,

and not be so small within

the sea in which we float

and forever spin.

We cry for our

beastly minds;

we are

blind.

New Testament

Spiders and Flies

Once there was a spider, Ariane, who sat at the hub of the webbed wheel of silk that she'd suspended across a wide fork in a tree branch. One day, she felt a tug from behind and glanced back to see a fat, struggling fly trapped in her sticky web. His wings were flapping up a storm to escape the gluey grip his legs were bonded in but, try as he might to pull away, Ariane's web held tight and true.

'Aha! A delicious treat has come a-wandering into my home!' cried Ariane, rubbing her limbs with glee. And she waltzed across the web, immune to its adhesion.

Looming over the hapless fly, her hungry eyes sparkling dark and eager, she said, 'Little fly, little fly – what a meal you'll make!' And she wrapped and wrapped him in her silk to hold him tight and save him for dinnertime.

'Well,' said the fly, with a tear in his compound eye, 'if I must be eaten, then it is an honour to be the meal of one as beautiful as you.'

'Beautiful? Me?' said Ariane, who blinked – once, twice – and now saw the rich hint of puce on the fly's head and the six beautifully slender legs extending from his chiselled abdomen and thorax.

'But, of course!' said the fly. 'Why, I could have been caught in the slimy tongue of a swamp toad, preyed on by a hunching mantis or clapped in the terrible beak of some scrawny bird. But here I am in the splendid web of the most wonderful spider in all the many metres I've travelled. I swear, twixt this tree and that brown one over yonder, there is no arachnid more radiant, more fair and more bootilicious than you. Why, you shake that abdomen as if it was soon to be out of fashion! Eat away, goddess of the web, you've earned it.'

Ariane shooed her embarrassment away with a spindly wave of her foreleg, 'Oh, what a little charmer you are! Such a way with words! If I knew no better, I'd say your lips were glossed with nectar, not excrement. But what else should I have expected from a fly with such shining eyes and such silky, flowing antennae?'

And Ariane and the fly, who was named Rodney (for his father), spent the warmer part of the afternoon laughing and swapping anecdotes from days gone by. Ariane leaned on her elbows and allowed herself to smile as Rodney listened and joked from inside his silky bondage. Rodney impressed Ariane with his daring adventures against the deadly swipes of the rolled-up newspaper – a villain that had seen the end of dozens of his siblings. Ariane walked Rodney through her web – how she'd planned its design and spent hours suspending and swirling it into a home she could be proud of. She was considering a dawn-facing extension so she could enjoy warm, lazy mornings. Rodney told Ariane how he'd heard legends of horses just beyond the way, and how every fly dreamed to crawl about in the lush moistness of their eyes. He'd always hoped to find a horse one day, but he knew that not all dreams could be realised.

As the sun finally fell beyond the horizon, they realised at the same moment that they were truly smitten. They were unable to break the gaze between their many eyes and could not deny the connection between them. They were meant to be.

Ariane released Rodney from his straitjacket and let him ride on her back so as to protect him from the tacky floor of her home. Together, they found the world a richer, more colourful place than it had been before, when they lived separate lives. Ariane had long lived a quiet existence of waiting and watching the world pass around her – she showed Rodney how to be a peaceful observer. Her patience was a magical quality – Rodney's mind unfurled to the sounds of the wind, the call of the birds and movement of the light around them. Ariane spoke so softly, allowing each of her words to live and breathe – so different from Rodney's hurried, chirrupy banter. Ariane struggled at first to keep up with his side of the conversation but, when she did, she realised how fast the world could move. Rodney darted high and fast, searching for food and mates as if each second was his last. He had no time to stop and smell the roses, but he saw so much more of the world than her: he could travel so quickly that he wasn't as troubled by the details as she was. He was a traveller.

They'd opened each other to the other side of the world. So intoxicating were their revelations that they were soon deep in each other's many arms: their legs intertwined, their labella locked and their eyes focusing only on the other. They had little care for the rest of the world – let them see! They wanted their love to be shared, to spill out and show the world what could be. Each day was a joy, walking arm-in-arm along the branches of the tree, watching the falling of the leaves or the 3 o' clock sun rays through the southern oak tree.

But nature did not look as kindly on them as they did on nature. They became the subject of sniggering insults as all the world, from birds to beetles, passed mocking whispers as Ariane and Rodney promenaded along their tree together.

The spiders were the first to confront them:

'What kind of filthy romance is this?' they said. 'How dare you play with your food like this, Ariane? Don't you know where it's been? Well, we can tell you exactly where it's been!'

'Come now, friends,' said Ariane. 'If you please, it is none of your concern what I do in my tree, in my web. A spider makes a home for her own spoils and, if I find companionship instead of dinner, then that business is mine alone.'

And the clutter of spiders was awash with the angry shaking of as many fists as they could manage without falling down. Their many eyes blinked in disbelief. An outsider might have thought they were at a spider rock concert, but no: something was very wrong.

Then the flies came buzzing furious from the sky in a cumulus of outrage.

'Rodney, you great winged sultana!' they said. 'Don't you see who that bladdy is? It's only the bladdy enemy! She'll bite your bleedin' head off before she falls in love with you, sunshine!'

'I know with whom I travel,' said Rodney. 'Ariane and I are together – we're happy in each other's company.'

'We don't bladdy care, Rodney! You're giving the kids the wrong idea – what if they all want to go swanning off with spiders?' Several among their number vomited their disgust. 'We'll all be bladdy doomed!'

'It's up to them,' said Rodney. 'Ariane and I have chosen to forsake the roles of hunter and prey to allow our love to burn bright! Our romance is ours alone and it won't cause you, or your children, to be swallowed up any sooner.'

And the flies shook their wings in outrage and rubbed their feet together in fury.

Ariane and Rodney carried on despite the protestations of their fellow creatures. Rodney, on Ariane's back, entertained Ariane with tales of life in the air; he described how the world pushed on forever above a quilt of trees and grass and water; how he ducked through branches and windows, dodging danger at every turn. And Ariane spoke of her private philosophical thoughts – a product of her silent, lonely life in waiting. She expressed her wonder at how green and brown everything seemed – how once she saw some scarlet on the breast of a bird, but it was gone oh so quickly. She had long tried to imagine how many colours may be hidden out there in the wider world.

And they contented in each other's company, their happy faces an anomaly among the red tooth and claw of nature.

The spiders and flies returned one night. Together they clamoured and boiled at the forsaken lovers, acid spittle frothing and bulbous abdomens wiggling. Ariane and Rodney looked out among them – how they mingled in tempestuous bile – with incredulity.

'You must end this abomination!' cried the spiders.

'Bladdy right!' said the flies. 'And if you don't, we'll tear you apart if we have to!'

'Please see sense, my friends!' cried Ariane, holding her head in her forelegs as if it might burst. 'Why can't we live in peace together?'

'It cannot be!' said the spiders. 'What you ask for is impossible.'

'Abso-bladdy-lutely! Spiders and flies getting along? Working together? You think you two can live in harmony or something? It goes against nature!'

'But look how you stand together now! Spider and fly, together as one!' said Ariane.

'Yes, can't you see? You prove yourselves wrong in your own anger,' said Rodney. 'If you are happy to be united in hate, then why condemn us, who are united in love?'

And the spiders and flies grumbled and stammered. They looked to one another and realised that they stood – shoulder-to-shoulder – with those they'd considered enemies. Hunters and their prey were fighting the same fight, no longer turned against each other.

And the flies started to wonder if the looks in the eyes of the spiders was anger... or hunger. Slowly, the attention of the crowd was turned away from Ariane and Rodney and onto one another as the reality of their strange intermingling dawned upon them. The flies chose not to test this strange truce any further than necessary.

'Well, we think we've made our point,' said the flies, and beat a hasty retreat.

The spiders were left alone with Ariane and Rodney, who held each other and looked out to the eights of eyes, still upon them.

'Perhaps any of us can find something in common,' said the spiders. 'Though we hope you never get hungry, Ariane.'

Ariane and Rodney were left alone in the half-moon light. They looked to one another, the last words of the spiders ringing between them in the silence.

'Care to dance?' asked Rodney.

'Delighted,' said Ariane.

And the two lovers span slowly on a dry, brown maple leaf as the stars shone upon them through the broken forest canopy.

The Libidinous List

Belinda Fontine awoke with the rough, acidic lick of tequila wringing her insides. This was most unusual for her; she was a woman who tended to treat herself to only a very occasional potent drink between lemonades. She'd allowed herself a wilder night to celebrate her birthday and the burning flames of intoxication had worked their way through her body to her mind; her memories of whatever jollies she'd enjoyed were now charred and broken.

She allowed her guide dog, Butters, to lead her down stairs, relying on her direction far more than usual. When finally she'd managed to set herself at the kitchen table with a stack of hot, buttered triangles of toast and a steaming mug of tea, she noticed Butters stifling a husky giggle.

'How much do you remember of your birthday night, Belinda?' Butters asked.

'Why?' asked Belinda pointedly. 'Is there anything that should spring to mind, Butters?'

'Only a certain someone, handsome, tall and charming, who most definitely had his eye on you.'

'Really?'

'Oh, yes. And a little more than his eyes were upon you, if I'm honest. You don't remember at all?'

'Goodness me – what did we do?'

'I saw a great deal of kissing and many wandering hands.' Butters laughed and panted. Belinda saw her faint blur of gold shimmer with her deep chuckles. 'None of your friends knew where to look, but you seemed very happy, I must say.'

Belinda flushed with embarrassment. Had she really made such a scene? The hair on her neck tingled a little as though her audience was still with her, gawking and pointing at her in her little kitchen. But, beneath her goose-pimpled skin, she warmed a little, knowing she'd had a passionate encounter – especially with a mysterious, handsome stranger!

Butters nudged a bone-shaped biscuit into her bowl of tea. 'I didn't expect him to get so carried away, but he definitely took a shine to you. And why wouldn't he?'

Through the red throb of her hangover, Belinda reached out to her mug of tea. She cradled it in both hands, feeling its soothing heat swim through her fingers. The clean, moist scent and the warm aroma of her toast entwined, lifting away her smouldering alcohol pains. She sipped the tea gingerly and was struck with a sudden thought.

'What on earth's wrong with me?' she said. 'If my head had been clearer, I could've given him my number and met him again.'

'Oh, Belinda,' said Butters. 'What kind of companion do you take more for? Of course I have his number for you – in my collar.'

Belinda ran her fingers under Butters's collar and found a rolled up scrap of paper.

'His name is Claude Blanc,' said Butters.

'Butters, you're an angel in wolf's clothing!'

Belinda was a busy woman these days. Finding a man to romance had become less of an adventure and more of a chore as time went by. She wasn't sure quite when the fun and excitement of dating had slipped away but somehow it had. Now she had to coax herself out to the singles' scene, where before she'd been fired by the compulsions of her flesh. Her once baby-smooth features had started to loosen – just a little – and she hoped she looked a little sprightlier than she felt. She'd spent far too long bobbing in the tides of traditional courtship, waiting for the perfect gentleman to fall heart-breakingly in love with her. Now she'd kissed a stranger on a whim and somehow it had reconnected her to the youthfulness she'd long been estranged from.

Butters read Claude's number aloud, while Belinda worked the telephone. She liked the pattern it made on her keypad; her fingers had to waltz to type it fast. She scratched Butters's head as the phone rang. When he answered, Claude's deep, purring voice brought fragments of memories floating to the surface.

'Hello Claude, it's Belinda from last night.'

He remembered her. And it didn't take him long to work out that he was faring better than she was.

'Oh, I don't know what you're talking about; I feel perfectly fine.'

Her grip on Butters's head tightened a little as she trotted out the little white lie. Hopefully she hadn't looked too much of a wreck when they parted.

'You know, I would love to.' A date. 'I'll definitely be able to survive a few cocktails.'

Once she was showered and dressed, she took the bus down to the noisy high street that was home to the noisy cocktail bar where Claude awaited them. Butters was no fan of buses or crowds, but, sensing Belinda's excitement, she kept her grievances to herself. It had rained recently and the scent of moisture was thick in the air as footsteps smack-smacked along the pavement. Butters led Belinda to the bar's entrance, where Claude greeted her warmly with a kiss to the cheek. She felt the spiky graze of his thin stubble.

By the time her first cocktail was half gone, she had realised with some certainty that Claude Blanc was not the type to hide his true self under the protection of veils and masks. She tended to find first dates to be slow-burning affairs, chit-chattering over silly subjects, circling tentatively towards zestier conversation. But he'd broken these expectations and caused her to choke on her fruit punch as he launched into the histories of his adventurous loins.

'There was one time when I slept with an octogenarian,' he said, tipping back his colourful cocktail. 'That might be the most interesting time I spent in a bedroom.'

For a moment, Belinda's mind seemed to disconnect itself from her tongue to save her from the hundred incoherent words that were bottlenecked at her throat and threatening to spill forth. She coughed awkwardly and tried to re-establish a little clarity. She'd felt uncomfortable for a moment, but he'd baited her and she found that she wanted more than the tempting little morsel he'd offered.

'It only *might* be the most interesting?' she asked, raising a curious eyebrow. 'And what other candidates are there?'

Claude leaned back, smiling, and began to walk her through his scattering of sexual encounters. He took her hands in his to better let her feel his body language and emphasis. By the end of her second cocktail she'd learned how many women had shared his bed ('Eighteen, which is a nice sort of number, isn't it, for a man of my age?'), his prophylactic lapses ('And she'd sat on it before I even knew what was happening!'); and how he had once failed his part in a threesome due to a terrible dearth of turgidity ('When there's three of you, there's always someone to watch you in action! I call it stage fright, Belinda!').

Despite the unusually blunt bent of conversation, Belinda found herself liberated by his casual charm and honesty. She happily shared her own lascivious abstract, including the tale of how she was once accidentally head-butted unconscious on one particularly passionate afternoon. She had not shared that tale with anyone.

With their bellies each four cocktails full, they left the bar and, waiting for Belinda's bus to arrive, they shared a long and lingering kiss. Belinda drank in the moment, hoping to fill the space left by the absent memories of their previous night. The chatter of townsfolk and the rush of traffic faded to near silence until she could hear only the heavy breaths escaping between their lips' intermittent embraces.

*

'So, Claude Blanc tells us he's not the relationship type,' Belinda muttered. She was sitting on the floor beside Butters's dog bed, her fingers wrapped around a mug of tea. Butters blinked through her sleepiness, licked Belinda's palm and wished her better luck with the next man.

'Men like Claude Blanc don't know how a lady should be treated. You're far too good for his kind,' she sniffed decisively.

'Oh goodness, Butters, I don't want a relationship with him,' said Belinda, chuckling. 'That'd be a tremendous disaster – I'm certainly not *that* blind. But then, to think of never seeing him again when he could open up a whole other world...'

Butters, her tail flicking her flanks, wondered if she might ever return to sleep. Squinting through the glare of her night light, she asked why she would ever want to see more of such a dead-end fellow.

'He intrigues me,' said Belinda.

She climbed into bed and lay with her fingers crossed over her chest, pondering where the road with Claude might turn, and where it would end. Could it really be so unthinkable to spend their shared existence entirely beneath the sheets? She had to allow her curiosity a little freedom. She called Claude the very next day.

For their next date, Belinda decorated her nudity with newly-purchased, bright pink underwear. She chose the kind that curved gently over her bottom and occasionally peeked its lacy edge over the waistband of her skirt, like a little wink to Claude. She hoped she looked alluring. She grabbed her walking cane and let Butters lead her into the night.

She tried to see if Claude could be diverted to non-erotic trains of conversation: personal ambitions; the beauty of the pyramids; how she mistrusted Jessica Fletcher. He was not to be swayed, though; with a casual double-entendre, an innuendo or a quick-witted segue into a personal anecdote, he was able to steer the topic back to his rampant sexuality with ease. Sometimes she didn't even realise it had happened until she was deep in debate with him about rather more delicate topics. Butters growled softly and pawed the carpet of the pub.

Claude brought them a bottle of ice-chilled wine from the bar. Before he had even fully sat down, he asked her, 'What do you think of ménages à trois?'

She laughed; he enjoyed toppling her composure. Could she imagine sharing the night with more than one partner? She hadn't ever considered it before, so she was curious to look inside herself to the opinion lying hidden there. She thought that, under certain well-laid conditions, she could well explore the idea.

'I like that you think that,' Claude said. His voice hummed with the pique of intrigue that Belinda had grown to recognise. And now they had ignited the idea of all the possibilities that awaited them, they batted teasing scenarios back and forth, trying to reveal the other's fantasies and limits. They fished for the daydreams that might have once, fleetingly drifted into their minds but had never been seriously expressed or considered. After cowering so long being the protective shield of her personal secrecy and reservation, Belinda was unshackled by revealing her innermost thoughts to this shiny, new man. She let thoughts escape that before had only drifted through her mind and roused her body at late, lonely bedtimes. The more Claude opened his ideas to her, the more she wanted to reveal in return. All the fantasies and eroticisms that she had previously attributed to harlots, whores and hussies - she realised that they all lived within her and she felt naked. It wasn't the mortifying nakedness of the bashful, either, but the intoxicating nakedness of a streaker. Though she would lie in the retelling, the truth was that she, not Claude, had inspired the idea of committing a fantasy agenda to paper.

'You know, Claude,' Belinda said, allowing her hands to stretch from his palms to his wrists and pull him to her. 'Now that we know so much about each other and what we dream about...why, there's no reason we can't try and bring some of those dreams to life.'

'There's a boldness in you I hadn't seen before,' said Claude.

'I'm a little surprised myself,' she whispered, and bit her lip. 'I have desires, Clause. And they're held back by nothing more than silly blushes. With you, what do I have to blush about?'

'Nothing at all.'

Belinda felt protected in their tryst. In their short time together, they could fulfil their secret desires before parting ways forever. They could charge their lives with their erotic imaginations and remain safe in each other's secrecy.

And so, in this bond of trust, they inked out their sexual manifesto. They filled a page with all the excitement they were willing to try together: moments they wished to share, reasons to lose hours in nudity, ways to find hidden pleasures. Butters wished she had the dexterity to cover her ears; instead she whimpered gently under the table in the hopes of blotting out their conversation.

Butters could not giggle as Belinda did. She did not smile or blush as the plan took shape, for she was a dog steeped in tradition: always the way with Labradors. Holding her snout high, she recalled the days of Belinda's old beau, Jeremy.

Jeremy was quite the gentleman. He and Belinda had stayed together for many years and Butters had watched them as they grew increasingly familiar with each other: how they liked their toast, Jeremy's red socks on Saturdays, Belinda's various little ways to make her blind life easier and Jeremy's kind consideration as he wordlessly worked them into his routine. Though they grew strong together, they were fractured by Jeremy's struggling business. Their mutual support was gradually replaced by a heavy friction that dragged and dragged until the tension had worn away all the happiness that had kept them together. After Jeremy left, Butters spent many weeks pacing the front window, waiting for his return. She knew he was gone forever, but she held onto her futile hope far longer than Belinda did.

Butters saw the world as a tapestry woven in golden thread: a fairy tale with princesses, bold knights and everlasting love. The sordid shenanigans she saw in late-night dance halls were a reason for her to bury her head in her paws.

Once Belinda and Butters were alone at home, the moping dog's discomfort was all the more noticeable to Belinda.

'You're scrabbling at crumbs because you think you can't find anything better,' said Butters.

'There are so many different types of relationship, Butters' said Belinda.

'And how will you feel in a year's time?'

'I couldn't possibly say.'

'What would your friends and parents think?'

'I don't need to discuss all of my choices with them.'

'Because you're ashamed.'

'Because my business is my own.'

'But what if you find yourself in love?' asked Butters.

With that, Belinda laughed. She broke and shuddered with mirth until her eyes were shiny with tears. How could she ever fall for a man who cared only for her flesh and not her heart? It was absurd beyond anything she'd ever concocted with Claude Blanc.

And so, their scheme took flight. At first, she and Claude met in the hours between sunlight, sneaking to her chamber past the weighty, black gaze from Butters's still and shining eyes. Shut up safely in her bedroom, they would press into the pillows, pull away their clothes, knock her jewellery from the nightstand and pull themselves to union. Their universe shrank to the space that encompassed them. Belinda kept her smile hidden: strung over Claude's bare shoulder, buried in his chest or crushed into the mattress. It was a glistening, stretched, animal smile.

They allowed themselves to grow accustomed to each other's bodies, rhythms and contours and, when they'd exhausted every twist of shape they could contort, they let their action spill out to the open world. Their skin was touched by the fresh, summer air as they danced an unclothed ballet between the brick walls of old alleys, their knees growing muddy among scattered orchard apples, their backs cold against the concrete, dark corners of high-rise car parks. Every night, they returned home bearing the mud, blood and bruise tattoos of their adventures and Belinda would awake the next day to find tiny stones still nestled in her skin and broken twigs buried in her ruffled hair. During one particularly passionate episode of lust-making, Belinda heard a nearby pair of grandmothers mistake her concertos of pleasure for migrating birdlife. She held her laughter in. Each night, as Belinda drifted to sleep, she could not relax her smiles as the memories of the days gone by washed over her.

But Butters was uncomfortable. She was far from used to any of this: keeping guard at the edge of the park while Belinda and Claude rocked against a tree and spending night after night away from Belinda's side. She fretted and paddled her paws into the ground, restrained by loyalty from making any further fuss. Nonetheless, Belinda noticed her quietness and was reminded of her faithful companion's words.

'But what if you find yourself in love?'

She shooed the warning away and returned her mind to the pleasures of passion.

There was an old shop on an uneven, red-paved street whose windows were permanently blanked out with thin, beige blinds. She and Claude stole into its short aisles of adult wares, giggling and delighting in its variety. They moved from the ethereal undergarments and nightgowns that weighed no more than smoke in her hands to libraries of erotic films, the titles of which reduced Belinda to a heap of giggling mirth. The shopkeeper watched them in the curved corner mirrors as they chuckled easily among the taboos with locked arms. As they browsed the curiously moulded plastic and rubber playthings, Belinda struggled to make sense of the shapes through the stiff packaging until the shopkeeper kindly helped her with some of the display models. She found some confusing, but most exciting. Some were quite simple, bulb-headed shafts; others looped, tangled, branched and quivered in extraordinary ways and, as Belinda fed them through her fingers, she delighted in deducing their orientation and purpose.

In the nights that followed, Butters could heard everything from behind Belinda's closed bedroom door as she lapped the warm cocoa from her bowl. Over the giggles and under the gasps, she heard soft mechanical hums: swarms of bees accompanying Belinda and Claude's ecstatic bird song and the percussive kicks of the headboard against the wall. Belinda woke each morning with a sparkle in her smile: her eyes beaming under a well-scruffed poof of hair, her now-slightly bow-legged walk keeping a bounce to its step. But as she stroked Butters a 'good morning' there was no familiar swish-swish of a golden tail against the carpet.

'But what if you find yourself in love?'

The moon had turned a full cycle since Belinda and Claude had inked out their wish list. They expanded their invitation to parties of similarly-minded pleasure-seekers, as the list dictated. Belinda's bare skin tingled in anticipation as her bedroom filled with the excited whispers of a carnal menagerie. There were shuffles as clothing was discarded and her mattress rolled and creaked as bodies poured on to the bed around her. She could feel the air grow hot as the players drew close...

She and Claude spent those nights happily playing part of a wider game of mixed permutations of people, twisted gracefully in sweat, with limbs curling through furrows of bed sheets. She drifted and swam as in an ocean; her ecstasy arched at the touch of fingers, toes and lips across the inches of her skin; voices called from a hundred directions, each second bringing with it a new experience. She had never felt so touched, so moved and so beautiful.

From the hallway, Butters disguised her unrest by gnashing loud squeaks out of her rubber carrot toy whenever the clicking heels and thumping soles of Belinda and Claude's companions shuffled in and out of the house. They all bent to stroke and scuff her, but she ducked her head and whined. Over breakfast, television and tea, she and Belinda spoke of work and music and news of the world as they always had, but Butters increasingly worked her conversation through tightened jaw. They ignored the naked, copulating elephants in the room.

'But what if you find yourself in love?'

Louder and louder, Butters words returned to Belinda's head. With every thrust of flesh within, with every warming foreign breath and bite on her neck and every tightened claw of fingers down her back, the most frigid doubt shivered her to pimpled-gooseliness. To fall in love would be a tragedy: the furthest of falls, a slippery slope to the trough of an unclimbable valley. For, after all the salacious acts they had performed in the comfort of their agreement, she could not allow Claude to enter her heart as deeply as he had entered her loins. She had exposed her body, but she wished to keep her soul secreted; she could not bear to have him so dangerously close.

She imagined him bound in a shirt and tie, meeting her parents or standing before all her friends and family at their wedding. Did she want to spend her life with someone who'd seen such a side to her, with whom she had bonded over purest animalism? Her aunts and uncles would ask how they met and she'd have to lie or find a bravery somewhere that she'd yet to witness inside herself. Could she live with Butters's uncomfortable, disapproving growl for the foreseeable future? She felt grubby, suddenly, like she was eating with unwashed hands.

Of course, her feelings for Claude were nothing close to love, but what if she turned? What if a moment sparked between them as they lay exhausted and sweaty in each other's arms? That spark could become a flame and consume them both before they were able to recognise its influence. And she'd be stuck with the shame of their origin.

So, Belinda Fontine met Claude Blanc for a coffee one cold, hazy morning. She made sure to choose the plastic-lidded takeway cups and rested her cane against her chair, instead of sliding it under the table as she normally might. After a few quiet sips to bitter her tongue, she called the curtain on their time together.

'I think we've taken this as far as I'm happy to,' she said, holding his left hand in both of hers, her fingers on his palm. It clenched for an instant and relaxed.

'Of course,' he conceded, his tone formal and flat. 'The time was bound come eventually.'

Butters's tail was wagging and her mouth was panting in a wide smile; Belinda caught the scent of happy dog breath in the air. Claude slipped a crumpled fold of paper into her hand.

'Our checklist. You're the better of us to keep it, I think.'

Belinda wondered if he was alluding to his playboy personality or her inability to read, but already he was shaking her hand, warmly but firmly. She realised that this was their first handshake together. How queer. He helped her erase his number from her phone and did the same with hers, so that when he left the table and Belinda, he was gone.

A few mornings later, Belinda was indulging in a thickly-jammed round of toast, with Butters's flank leaning against her leg. Belinda was pleased to note that she had relaxed her growl and loosened her posture. Grilling up a second granary slice, she wondered if her heart could ever truly have fallen for that unabated rogue, Claude Blanc. It had been her fear; his audacious charm and unrestrained honesty had certainly hooked her in. But in truth, she had only ever fancied him as the key to her own liberation. He was a holiday, not a home; he was a wonderful tourist destination, but not someone she would ever have been able to live with. Her fear had entangled her thoughts and now he was gone, forever lost.

Leaving the bread to brown, she grabbed her large, leather bag and made her way to her bedroom. From the bag, she removed the crinkled list that Claude had left in her custody. She recalled the list by heart and, though she could not read it, she knew the one fantasy that remained uncrossed. She repeated it over to herself silently, allowing a smile to pull wide over her face. She held the paper tightly in her fist, as though the ink could flow into her body and give her the strength she had gained in her adventuring with Claude. Silently, she folded the list one, twice, and rehomed it out of sight in her nightstand drawer. There was plenty of time, and plenty of men, she thought.

Then she grabbed a slice of toast and took Butters for a walk in the clear morning air.

Falsify

If somebody claimed that the moon's run by trout,
We could fly someone up there, and they'd check it out.
But to posit that Santa employs teams of elves,
Could we really go and see this for ourselves?

You think that there might be a growth in your neck?
That's not very hard for the doctors to check.
But to feel there's a soul, nestling inside your heart?
Tell me how your investigation would start!

There's a way that we know all the things that we know,
We predict what a premise would probably show,
And then make a test to be sure it's correct,
If not, well, too bad, but it's best that we checked.

You think that they like you for your busty chest?
The hard part's constructing a trustworthy test.
But it can be done: simply match boobs to zeal,
For a large range of women – that'd be the ideal!

But to show there's a God who's outside time and space,
How can you do that when this God's left no trace?
For here is the secret to the art of testing:
It can only be done on those things manifesting!

For if something can alter the world that we know,
The effect of this 'something' needs testing, and so,
Without interactions we're able to measure,
We can dismiss something's whole existence at our leisure.

So you see if you say that pure milk can cure cancer,
There are trials we can run that will help find the answer,
But profess that you know where we go when we die
Well, you'll find that your premise deserves no reply.

Modesty Bryster and the Boobs of Destiny

There once was a woman named Modesty Bryster, whose breasts were as minimal as canvas freshly stretched over her willowy frame. This absence of overhang had not particularly bothered Modesty, whose dreams lay in bakery and bibliophilia. Since she was little, cradled in the arms of her mother and father, she'd always wanted to own a bookshop where she could also sell muffins, cakes and other sweet treats. From her youthful years, spent buried in stories and histories, she'd realised that nothing accompanied a good read better than a muffin or two on which to nibble.

But when the time came to fulfil her dreams, and she sought out the banker, he would not fill her purse. She went to the baker but he would not bake her muffins. She went to the bookman but he would not entrust to her his hardbacks. She sought out the counsel of the Mayor, an elderly man who had long looked over the growing town as a keen gardener would his hedgerow: with pernickety fuss and loving attention. But the Mayor, while keen on new enterprise, turned down her request for help as he called her venture 'a journey into the frivolous, with no hope of success.' The words stung Modesty more keenly, knowing as she did that, over the previous weeks and months, he had aided the foundation of Busty Barbara's All Milk Brasserie, D-Cup Danielle's Chicken Rodeo and Top-Heavy Tessa's Grow-Your-Own Steakhouse. *No, no, no*, thought Modesty crossly, *this rejection has little to do with success and everything to do with my chest!*

She knew why she was four-times rejected; why she was always shunned and looked-over – the blame rested solely on the petiteness of her bosom. Her curves were slight and this gave her plains where others bore mountains. Her nipple lacked the ambition to climb higher, her breasts had plateaued in their quest for a bolder topography and, with such a relaxed attitude so evident from her chest, no wonder others expected so little from the rest of her.

'Oh, my Boobs!' she cried out in anguish. 'Why must you drag the rest of me down to your lacklustre standards? Why must you project such lethargy upon me?'

'How very dare you!' said her Boobs, in piqued retort. 'Do not be so rude as to hold us responsible for your own lack of progress!'

'My Boobs! You argue so?' said Modesty. She was confused and held them in crossed palms as one might if caught in the nude.

'Indeed we do! Are we not a part of you? Do we not fall as you fall, climb as you climb? Are we not part of your care, as your eyes and stomach and feet unquestionably are? If you leave your feet unwashed and uncared for, so that they rot and dissolve and leave you unable to walk do you cry to them, "Oh, Feet, how you disappoint me so!"? No indeed, for you know you must nurture and understand your feet if you wish to walk far in this world.'

'But, Boobs, you know I can nurture you no further,' said Modesty, aghast at the accusation. 'As a woman, I am as grown as I can be. Just as I can grow no taller, your form is set as a part of me: a muffin baked is a muffin shaped.'

And her Boobs chortled in their unnecessary brassiere, and said, 'Your knowledge is slight – there are things abundant in this world that can change the things you think are unchangeable. We can guide your success, as there is no wisdom like the wisdom of the bosom. Help us, and we will help you. Feed us the sweet blossom from the coparelleno tree and, in return, we promise to advance your life to where it should be.'

So Modesty ventured out to the corner of town, where the cobble-stone paths faded to mossy dirt tracks and cultivated farmland broke to wild and wicked grassland. She walked to where the earth sloped down to the edge of the woods, where the coparelleno trees grew. She picked the blossom from the ends of their branches and fed it to her Boobs until they were satisfied.

The next morning she woke to a slightly larger bosom upon her torso.

'My Boobs, you have filled a little!' she elated, pulled her nightgown from her nudity. 'See how I can create a faint line between you if I push you thus. A cleavage, my Boobs, a real cleavage!'

'As we promised you, my dear – we came to your aide! Now, off to town and let us acquire that bookshop!'

And so, Modesty Bryster sewed and tightened her brassiere to force her Boobs to a cleave, popped open an extra button on her brightest pink top and departed to the banker, the baker and the bookman. Oh, she told them again of her great plans of muffins and literature! She smiled and joked and expressed her dearest desires. Their attention was caught in her fierce grasp and this time they were truly rapt!

To her joy, Modesty secured a little bookshop in the old tinker's place at the end of the main parade. She decorated it in wood and stone and painted ceramic and the people soon came to read and nibble, albeit slowly and warily. Most folks were loyal to their bakers and their booksellers but a few began to pass through and spend their elevenses with a hardback that thrilled them with tales of adventure and misdeeds. But Modesty had hoped for more. She had poured years of gold savings into her efforts and she would be dead before she saw that gold again she could not attract men, women and children by the cartload. She slumped by the warmth of the oven.

'Why is custom as slow as treacle on a winter's day when the coffee shop yonder sees drinkers queuing by the dozen? It can't be owt but the explosive bust of the barista, a splendid sight indeed when compared with my forced efforts.'

Her Boobs awoke with two pokes and a shiver, and said, 'We are always able to come to your service, my dear – in exchange for the sweet blossom of the coparelleno tree.'

So Modesty returned to dark, damp corner of the world where the coparelleno trees grew tall and fed its blossom to her hungry Boobs. When they were sated once more, she retired to her cottage and slept. When she awoke, she was further endowed and plumpened of breast.

'My Boobs!' she enthused, cupping each with a palm. 'Look at the ballast you carry at last! Look how now I bear the shadow of underboob – a pair of slight, but noticeable smiles!'

'Indeed, it's true,' her Boobs replied. 'Now – out, into the world and claim what's ours!'

And so Modesty took off into town and purchased fanciful new lingerie, laced and contoured to handle and flatter her new physique. And as the muffins baked and rose in their cups, Modesty welcomed in passers-by from the street with samples and tasters. She propped open the door to let passers-by see her curves and smell her baking. Her shapely balcony proudly abundant, she called:

'Comfort yourself among marvellous books with delicious treats! Make yourself at home, peruse, graze and relax!'

And so they flocked, those crowds of folks; taking tales and leaving crumbs. The money began to pile up within the safe, forcing Modesty to increase the frequency of her journeys to the bank teller. She began to tickle inside, thinking of how she had been able to bring folk into her shop with her new found power. She laid a hand upon her bosom and wondered: was there more she could do than force the ebb and flow of citizens to her little shop? A thought sparked in her mind and caught aflame in the aether:

'My Boobs,' she said, 'I wish to oust the Mayor. He has sat at the head of this great town for far too long a spell, hanging like the sad branches of a weeping willow, casting a shadow over the rest of us. His ways are old and stubborn; we should round up the people in rebellion against him! Is it possible?'

'It may indeed be possible, Modesty, with our help of course,' said her Boobs, with a momentary jiggle. 'But only if you feed us the sweet blossom of the coparelleno tree. Quid pro quo and tat for tit!'

So, once again, Modesty stole out to the coparelleno trees and plucked the blossom in the mauve of twilight. She fed her Boobs till they were sated and retired to her cottage to sleep. When she awoke in the morning she found a heaving softness weighted upon her chest.

'My Boobs!' she cried. 'How large and round you have become! I'd be bold enough to declare you a handful each and, though my hands are small and dainty, this is impressive beyond my expectations!'

'We promised you change, my dear, and we delivered,' her Boobs replied. 'Now, out in to town with you! Let us inspire the people!'

So Modesty stood tall at the statue in the centre of the old town square. Her figure was more curvaceous than they could remember seeing upon her; her bosom flesh lifted and cradled by careful turns of fabric and seam. Not a person passed her by who did not turn a glance her way or stop to hear her cry. She saw the attention she had never before attracted and suppressed a smile, keeping her face serious and dignified.

'Good people!' she cried. 'For too long we have lived with the old Mayor's miserly grip on this town. Now, it is up to us to take a stand, I say! One and all, we must take this moment and send him scampering from his high office. What say each and all of you?'

The crowd cheered: Hurrah! Hurrah! Buoyed by Modesty – and her mighty mammries pointing the way - they punched their fists in the air and followed her all the way to the Mayor's office. Soon they were rioting up a storm, kicking dust into the air and chanting songs of hope and revolution. Too old and frightened to contend with the revolt, the Mayor donned his hat, hopped through the back door and escaped over the horizon. The people roared in triumph and lifted Modesty Bryster over their shoulders, placing her reverently in the mayoral seat.

'You wish for me to sit as your Mayor?' she asked.

Yes, they cried, for she had warmed them and inspired them. Now she would lead them!

When she sat, finally alone at the polished mahogany grain of the old mayor's desk, she crinkled her brow to a ripple of worry. The desk seemed so large and the office so small. So many voices had cheered her name; so many eyes looked up at her office windows.

'Oh, now what shall I do? I don't know how to champion a town,' she whispered.

'Fear not, my dear.' Her Boobs spoke up. 'We can help you again; we are wise to the ways of leadership, you'll see. First, of course, you must feed us more of the sweet blossom of the coparelleno tree...'

And so Modesty took the blossom once more and fed it to her Boobs till they were full and comforted. The next morning, as she had grown to expect, she had changed once again. What once hung as mangos were now very much melonous. So large they were that it took Modesty a heave to sit up from her bed – a heave she was not used to. Her balance was strange and the weight of the Boobs added a certain momentum to her step as she walked around her cottage.

'Oh, my Boobs! How hefty you are upon me!'

'Indeed!' said her Boobs. 'All the better to lead you onward. And now, Modesty, let's take the reins of this town and charge onward!'

And Modesty seemed to know how to act without thinking. Words and actions passed through her mind as easily as breath through her lungs. She spoke with an oratory that would set her words in stone for generations. She penned charters and notices that coddled the town's contentment. She spoke with leaders across the land. The town was run like a dance; every step flowed to the next – though she felt, at times, intoxicated by its melody. Her aptitude for leadership had come so naturally, as effortlessly as falling to sleep.

And at the dark of each day, she satisfied her Boobs with the blossom from the coparelleno tree, without even waiting to be asked. Why, she barely gave it a thought or notice, so rutted in her routine it was. And her Boobs grew larger still – inviting, squashy pillows of cleavage – until they were the finest and deepest in town. The greater her bosom became, the easier she found her mayoral duties. Life continued in this lazy state until, one day, Modesty awoke and realised her body was engaged in business without her. It showered without her, dressed without her – low cuts and high skirts – breakfasted without her and headed off to the mayor's office without her. Modesty was trapped inside her own body!

'Alas, I am not the mistress of myself!' she cried.

'No, indeed,' said her Boobs, 'we have taken control, now. You may sit and watch; let us work on your behalf.'

'But I do not wish to yield control!'

'But so you did, now hush and be calmed.'

And the Boobs, as Modesty Bryster, continued to pull the town together as a mighty force. They all were one – a township, a community, a people! But gently, surreptitiously, the Boobs' words turned from motivation to anger. Words of pride and reclamation slipped into speeches, ideas of war and demonstration were littered through declarations. The townsfolk were more than collected – they were furious for more. The Boobs fed them notions of inadequacy in the shadow of neighbouring towns and cities. It was time to set things right and show the other people of the world just what the town could achieve. Against the silent, internal protestations of Modesty Bryster, the Boobs led the town to war.

By the fading light, the Boobs fed on the blossom of the coparelleno tree; by the fiery dawn they sent out the citizens to do battle with neighbouring settlements. The word was war. Surrender, and be consumed by a new beginning, or fight and be consumed by fire. The Boobs and the town that followed them showed no mercy. So persuasive and so charismatic were the Boobs that many towns laid down their arms and joined with the invading party. Very few settlements stood to battle; some out of fear, most out of awe.

The Boobs and the town set to a mighty task – the great logistical and architectural feat of establishing a new capital city. They would build a majestic tower in the centre of town on the site of the once humble mayor's office. Conquered towns submitted their resources: timber, coal, metal, stone and labour – all eager to be a part of the great tower. The structure grew as a patchworked twist of broken buildings and materials, with each town bringing its own style to the task. The metals came from burned out buildings, reshaped farming tools and weaponry, the wood from oak and maple and beech, the stone torn from old barns and walls. The shadow of the great tower stretched out over the people below, visible for miles. It was an ugly thing: twisted, leaning and dark. It moved in the wind and creaked in the cooling of the evening. The floors were uneven and split, the walls sometimes as thin as glass.

Modesty continued to hear tales of the multitudes who had fallen at the blades and arrows of the invading army. She cried out to her Boobs with unbearable heartache:

'But, no – there cannot be violence from me! This was never what I wanted; this is never what I dreamed! My dreams were of books and muffins and comforting things.'

'Be still, be silent,' said the Boobs. 'We are stronger without you.'

And the Boobs gorged on the blossom of the coparelleno tree.

Until one day, things were different. From the top of the monstrous rickety tower, Modesty stood to address the waiting army at its foundation. The monument creaked from its spine as a morning breeze swept by and Modesty steadied herself. The Boobs, engorged and bulbous, were oversized and disturbed of shape, as though two pumpkin seeds had been planted beneath her flesh, long ago. They were larger than heads, heavier than the rest of her with nipples that punched like absurd purple fists from the hardened skin. Her clothes were ripped, sewn and re-sewn to keep the Boobs contained and comfortable. The crowd were blind to her ludicrousness no longer.

'You are a farce of bosomery!' said a voice from the front. 'A farce, I say!'

'An unholiness of oompahpah!' said another.

The crowd began to jeer and yell, laugh and cry. They pointed and shook their fists, gesturing in mockery as a relief swept over them and the fever of a multitude broke out. She was a clown: a malformed insanity beyond all humanity. And when they had laughed all the spirit from their lungs, they disbanded to their homelands and left Modesty and the Boobs alone.

Suddenly, in the weakness and hesitation of abandonment, the Boobs momentarily lost their grip over Modesty. Seizing the moment, Modesty pulled a sword from the wall of the tower. With a fierce scream, she cut the Boobs from her body.

They fell from her, plummeting from the peak of the tower to the dirt that held its foundations. Modesty heard them screaming all the way down like fireworks until, with a heavy thud, they were still. Peeking down, she watched as the Boobs lay still in dusty craters, staring back at her with scowling, frowning nipples. The Boobs were no more!

Modesty took hold of her weakened body. Tentatively, she began to climb down the shivering, skeletal tower, taking each step with slow attention – partly because the floors were weak and splintering, but mostly because she preferred the loneliness and shame to the ridicule that would surely come. She kept climbing down, though, holding on to what she could and testing the floors and footholds. How ever would she live? With the shame of a fallen campaign and less bountiful breasts than ever before, what hope did she have of success now?

The floor became sturdier as she continued her descent; ladders and rope nets gave way to stairs – real stairs! The creaking of the tower became quieter with every step and she no longer needed to hold on to the walls with both hands to steady herself. A thought came to her: what had the Boobs really done for her? Certainly, they had grown, but had they granted her skills? They'd been charismatic when they finally possessed her but, before then, were they not just decoration? And were people so shallow to give so much to someone with a little more plumpness to their chest?

She was nearing the bottom of the tower now. She was walking quickly and freely through its jumbled maze, unhurried by the fear of collapse. Maybe she had brought the good things upon herself – the books and the muffins, the custom and gold. Perhaps she'd been looking in the wrong places for change.

Finally, Modesty emerged from the base of the tower and stepped out into its shadow. The solid earth felt good under her feet. She was haggard and exhausted, but happy. She shuffled across town, keeping quietly to herself, and when she reached her bookshop, she saw a crowd of impatient, waiting people standing at its door for Modesty, the exuberant, baking bookworm to welcome them in for muffins, books and old-fashioned comforts.

The Immortal

In a world a little different from our own, all people were governed by one woman. Her name was Gia Panta. To speak of her would cause all the organs in your body to loop-de-loop, your nerves to quicken and your jaw to clamp, for she was truly the most powerful being that history had ever witnessed.

She had gained ascension on a tide of tremendous bloodshed. Warriors and soldiers had fallen in her wake; the ashes of cities smouldered in her passing; her armies of beasts and birds shielded her from death, striking her enemies and absorbing their strikes. Never before had an individual snatched sovereignty over the Earth, and yet Gia Panta had taken it with such cool arrogance. People spoke in hushed huddles of how nation after nation had bowed a reluctant surrender and thrown down their weapons in reverence to Gia Panta; of how she had united the globe as one people, dispelling the idea of 'nations' and dictating the people to her whim.

And though the people never lost their fear of Gia Panta, their bitterness towards her began to fade, and then to sweeten. She did not treat them as slaves, but saw each of them as a powerful part of a great machine: the human race. She lusted for innovation and invention, yearning for discovery and knowledge and pushing humankind in the direction of investigation and engineering. She wished to see how far the human race could stretch itself, what it could achieve and what magnificent secrets it could unlock from the universe's mysterious fabric. Gia Panta oversaw cities that rose like sun-drenched wheat in previously barren lands; wondercrafts – with and without occupants –that reached out into the heavens and explored the vastness beyond; energies that could be harvested and consumed in quantities previously unimaginable. The human race flowed together as one, drawing oars of invention and pulling swiftly and without fear through a sea of enlightenment.

Of course, this was not always the case; there were some who rose up rebel against Gia Panta's dictatorship. But she destroyed them easily and without mercy; she was as fast as any challenger, accurate beyond belief and devastating in her retribution. Into the walls of the capitol building, she chiselled the names of those who fell at her hand as a warning to those who continued to harbour dreams of rebellion.

Eventually, her opposition dwindled in the luxury of her prosperous empire. All who had lived in the time of her ascension grew old and died. And she lived on at the throne of the Earth, watching centuries pass and generations go by. She saw the population crowd and ebb; she saw men and women grow tall; she watched technology pour into her tiny telephone until she could look out on all the world through its tiny screen.

For a time, some on Earth had begun to treat her as a God, but she refused and forbade their worship. She insisted that she was a human like any of them and that they should treat her accordingly. The people took her at her word, though they could not understand how someone so small, slight of muscle and tinged with the frailty of humanity could rise to take the world as her own, guarding it for centuries and shooing away death as an insufferable fly.

As further centuries passed, Gia Panta felt content to loosen her grip on the world and leave it in the hands of the people themselves. Instead of ruling, she chose to walk among them as a quiet observer. Still fascinated by their technologies, she stopped by their laboratories and observatories to inquire about their latest discoveries. She still carried all her power in their presence, so could pass where she wished, like a ghost through walls.

It was in the agency of interstellar exploration, a millennium since her assumption, that she found herself a lover. She saw the passion in the eyes of the professor, Robin, and realised she could never be parted from it. And so they became lovers, partners, and friends. The two of them were inseparable and, the stronger their love burned, the less Gia cared to control the world.

And one day Robin asked Gia, 'My love, how is it that you live so long, that you can give and take as you desire, that you could take the world and shape it like clay?'

And Gia answered, 'My dear Robin, if I tell you my secret, will you promise to take it for yourself, with all the risks and the tragedy that accompany it, and come away with me to the stars, forever?'

'Anything, dear lover.'

'Then I shall tell you.' Gia cleared her throat. She seemed afraid, as though her secret was laced with a deadly poison that she would be unable to control. 'You are aware of the hypothesis of the multiverse, Robin?'

'But of course, Gia. It assumes that every interaction that occurs in this universe has its alternate outcome played out in another, separate universe.'

'So a die that rolls a six here might roll a four in another world, you see.'

'I'm not convinced if you could allow it that latitude, dearest Gia,' said Robin, with a kind curiosity.

'Oh but you can, Robin. And I am the proof. For I took it upon myself to test the idea with my own life. Do you see? If I die in one world, I live on in another, none the wiser to the death of my alternate. Somewhere, I must always live on; I must always be successful. In one world, I will always win the battle, where my alternates fall. If you are willing to take the risks that accompany the challenge of seizing the planet for your own, you will do it, somewhere.'

'But Gia, darling...'

'Yes, I have died a million – even a billion – times. I have sacrificed my own, alternative lives, countless times over. There were countless universes in which I was quickly snuffed out, overthrown, tortured, arrested, injured and worse. I sacrificed those lives for this one, in which I live on forever. I am sure, even as we speak, I am dying of extreme age somewhere. I wonder which Gias embrace that death and which fear it. I'm sure the Gias that met you will wish to live on.'

'And you wish me to make these same choices?'

'I already know you will.'

'You can't be sure.'

'Somewhere, in some world you will make that choice. I can afford to be arrogant, because I know that it will reward me somewhere.' Gia smiled so slightly that Robin wondered if the expression was conjured entirely in imagination.

And so Robin took Gia by the hand and vowed to stay with her at the expense of disaster for an infinite number of elsewhere Robins.

One day, they built a ship for themselves and left the Earth behind to take the reins of its own destiny. And, fearless, they pulled back the curtain of stars to explore the world beyond.

The Grand Designer

A shirt is designed by a tailor,
A painting's designed by an artist,
So beautiful beings like humans,
Are designed, then, by one of the smartest?

So the wonderful weather, like rainfall,
And trees that spread leaves out to sunbeams,
Are the products of someone's great paintbrush:
A painter whose skills are supreme.

But if houses and cars and we people,
And dogs, peas and dirt are designed;
If design is implied from all details,
Then how can design be defined?

So if designed things have all been designed,
And all things undesigned have design,
Then designed things: designed; non-designed things: designed,
By a mind whose design is divine.

If designs that designed the 'designed',
Were designed by a kindly Designer.
Who designed the Designer designing,
The designed, non-designed and designers?

The God from the Clay

There was a very dirty man in the middle of a field. He had soil rubbed into his sleeves, dirt caked over his long johns, and his face – well, suffice it to say that only the clean trails of sweat that crossed his brow gave any hint to the true colour of his skin. The man's name was Brian and he was sitting at the edge of a hole in the earth that he'd spent the best part of a week excavating. He'd found a few small bones that he suspected to be the toes of a dinosaur and, if his predictions were correct, the surrounding area would be abundant with ancient life.

Swinging his legs over the edge of the hole and chewing thoughtfully on a fish sandwich, Derek gently turned one of the fossils over in his hand. He was anxious to return the toes for examination but there was still much work to be done in the earth.

'Hello, young man. I was wondering if you could answer a few questions...'

There was a man lying at the base of his dig. He looked as old as the fossils that surely lay beneath him; he was built like a vine, with not a morsel of meat on him; he was naked, his modesty spared by the long, white beard that wrapped around his torso. Smiling up at Derek, this nude grandfather figure was surprisingly content for someone planted firmly in such wet muck.

'No?' continued the man. '*One* question, then? You can hear me?'

'Yes, I can hear you,' said Brian, the last bite of fish sandwich still dissolving in his stunned mouth. 'What on earth are you doing down there? Where did you come from?'

'Questions of your own,' said the man. 'I see. Well, let's play a game then. We each earn the right to ask a question if only we answer one first. How about that? I'll answer first: I am lying in a ditch, young man. Now it's your turn to answer one of my questions.'

Standing on his bony legs, the man stretched to full height and looked out over the landscape beyond the ditch. His eyes shone with moisture, though Brian was unsure if the man was overcome or if his eyes were simply reacting to the stinging chill of the breeze.

'What do you think of all this?' asked the man.

'What do I think of what?'

'Everything! All of this: isn't it wonderful?'

'Everything...' said Brian carefully to the strange naked man standing in his excavation, 'is wonderful. Yes. Just wonderful.'

'Excellent!' said the old man, leaping from the hole with an energy that made Brian wince. 'I was hoping you'd say that, because – well, let's not get ahead of ourselves... Your turn to ask a question.'

'Just who are you?'

'Ah, well that is exactly the right question to ask, young man.' The man tugged at the scruff of his beard, as if tweaking a bow tie. 'I am the creator of all things. The universal gardener, if you will.'

Brian swallowed. 'You're telling me that you're God?'

'My, my, my,' said God, pulling at the grubby skin at Brian's cheeks. 'Aren't you a thing of beauty? Everything's turned out ever so well.'

Brian was struggling to keep up with this strange old man and his many musings and, to make things more baffling, the God was suddenly buttoned into a three-piece pinstripe suit.

'You know, it's been far too long since I visited this place,' God mused, watching a flock of swallows roll across the sky. 'The last I saw you, you were still little single-celled things, floating about in the oceans. And now, look at you! So tall and...meaty!' he beamed.

Growing concerned for the clearly confused old man, Brian decided to lead him to the nearest town, where he might be able to find a doctor to care for him. He pointed to the roofs and chimneys that peeked out from over the shrubbery at the end of the field.

'What a marvellous idea, Brian! Let's get stuck in!' God rubbed his hands together in glee. 'But why walk, when we can fly?'

And before Brian could so much as grab his hair in frustration, the clouds themselves reached down to Brian and God, scooped them from the ground and whisked them across the mile of rain-soaked earth, over the hedgerow and into the town. They landed neatly at the crossing of two busy streets; the aromas of bread, meat and fish mingled in the air, mixed by a heavy traffic of bag-laden shoppers battling along the pavements. As Brian and God descended from the sky, the people froze in astonishment.

'You really are God,' said Brian, his legs wobbling a little beneath him.

His skin shining a little brighter than the winter sun should allow, God touched Brian affectionately on his crown. 'Why ever would I lie?'

And so, gathering around God and Brian, the crowds held their arms aloft and shouted their joyous and fearful proclamations in such frenzy that only the loudest voices could be picked from the hubbub.

'I knew you'd return!'

'I prayed to you every night!'

'Thank you, O Lord!'

'I'm sorry for my wickedness! I'm ever so sorry!'

And God kept quiet and listened to their flurry and bluster. They did not even notice that he had not said a word, so eager were they to speak out and declare themselves. Brian was stressed and intimidated by the thousands of voices growing stronger and more numerous by every passing minute, but God's serenity was unbroken and his smile unflinching.

In a moment too sudden for coincidence, the crowd fell quiet. Passing through a parting in the swarm was a short man draped in green and white robes, his gait brisk and his cheeks flushed crimson. It was the priest from parish at the crest of the town.

Reaching the front of his flock, the priest fell to one knee before God and cried out, 'O Lord, I came as soon as word reached me. I fall humbly before you and offer you sanctuary within the walls of my church.'

'Lead the way, kind sir,' said God, with a curious chuckle in his voice.

With Brian at his side God followed the priest as he led them through the crowd and up the hill to where the stone steeple of the church towered proudly over all around it.

'I must say, Brian,' said God, in a delighted whisper, 'In all the planets I've seeded with life, I've never one to ever have knowledge of me. I hardly have the time to make frequent visits to any particular place, what with the entire universe to tend to and what not. And yet, here, they cry out for me!'

'I'm really glad you're so happy with everything,' said Brian, his brow furrowing. 'But–'

'They worship me! They revere me, Brian. They thank me. I've never once been thanked for all my efforts; I considered creation satisfaction in itself, but to find other so pleased and thankful for it... well. That's something else altogether.'

'True, but –'

'Listen to their cheers, Brian, their nervous whispers and their hushed awe. That commotion is for me, Brian – for me!'

'I know, and it sounds great,' said Brian, pinching the bridge of his nose. 'But I'm a little concerned that you're not the God they think you are.'

'Nonsense, Brian! What other gods could there be? I would know – I created everything.'

'I'm speaking more of the God of the Bible, really.'

'The what?'

'And here we are!' said the priest. They were standing at the tall, wooden doors at the entrance to the grey stone church. The priest fumbled with his keys until they clanked into the lock and opened the way to the chilly interior. As he led them in and closed the door behind them, Brian heard a collective, disappointed sigh from the following crowd.

The priest offered them seats in the front pew and stood before them, his hand shaking and his voice dry.

'Tell me true, O Lord, are these the end times come at last?'

'The end times?' God's eyes narrowed and his face tilted.

'He's asking if you've returned to destroy the world, I think,' said Brian.

'Tell me, priest, why ever would I do that?' said God, leaning towards the priest and frightening him back a few paces.

'Isn't it obvious?' The priest looked nervously from God to Brian, terrified to give an erroneous reply. 'I mean, the world is a fallen place – so full of misery and terrible things. Oh, some of us have tried – and tried hard, believe me – to keep everything from collapsing, but now I see we've failed. I knew, in my heart, that it was only a matter of time before you'd come.' His mouth pursed with a quiver.

Fixed into the piercing grey of the priest's troubled gaze, God stood and rocked from one heel to another with the perilous gravity of a great stone boulder. The priest's words froze in his own throat as he panicked at God's sudden turn from delight to pensiveness. God nodded knowingly at the priest and, with his hands crossed at the small of his back, began to walk the length of the aisle, flooded in the stained light of the mosaic glass. He put a hand on the church door and paused, saying, 'I'll be but a moment.'

God closed the door behind him and stood before the quietly chanting crowd at the gates of the church. He contemplated them in silence for a few seconds as they watched him with greedy eyes. The fall of twilight had tinted their faces with a fiery mauve and God considered his own appearance through their eyes: their praise had given him a sense of importance he had not felt before, but now he wondered whether this place was world of failure.

'Hello,' God said, sitting on the stone steps of the church, crossing his legs under his knees and letting his toes play in the weeds. 'I'd like to ask a few questions, if you'll indulge me.'

The crowd stirred. Hums and murmurs rippled through their number.

'Have you heard of the end times?'

The murmurs ceased. Each and every pair of eyeballs shot a look of fear.

'Answer me honestly, my people,' said God. 'Do you think the world deserving of an end? Do not fear speaking truthfully – this is your chance to speak your mind.'

The silence drifted by before a man at the front of the crowd began to clear his throat. 'We were worried it would be too late,' he said. 'We thought the wickedness would overcome us all before your return and none of us would be worthy of salvation.'

'Tell me of this wickedness,' said God. He preferred the unapologetic praise, but an honest criticism was just as strange and poignant. He could fix things. He could make them love him again.

'There is murder,' said the man. 'People who snuff out the lives of others, selfishly and angrily, leaving the bereaved in their wake.'

God considered this. 'These people are the unkempt edges of my otherwise beautiful shrubbery. I can prune back these untidy edges and make this world perfect again, you will see – you will be happy again.'

And God launched out onto the world, flying over every continent and dropping tremendous stones from the skies to crush and smite every man, woman and child who had ever sought to end a human's life. The streets were strewn with the broken corpses of the wicked and, when God returned, the crowd sang and prayed for him.

And God was happy once more, but a woman spoke out from the crowd: 'But what of those people who steal sex from the vulnerable? What about the horrible, despicable people who use strength and charm and fear to force their power upon the sex of others. These misdeeds are surely as ruinous as those of the murderers?'

God agreed that this was a serious desecration of his great creation and so he launched out over the world once more. He folded wildcats from the shadows to hunt down the sexual predators. The beast flew out and ripped the meats from their bones until their skeletons lay shattered and bloody in the dust. God returned once more to the cheering, jubilant crowd.

But still there was disquiet among the people. Growing in their eyes was the light of realisation. God truly had returned and it was time to make the Earth holy again. This wasn't the end of times – it was the new beginning.

They spoke fiercely of the doctors and would-be parents who scoffed at God's plans for life and destroyed life at its most precious and vulnerable – in the womb. God plucked the squandered brains of the doctors from their skulls and rendered pregnant wombs impenetrable, but this was not good enough. The people told him of the men and women who sought to blunt the miracle of child creation even before fertilisation with pills and rubber to indulge in their own depravities and forgetting God's great design for partnership. And after God destroyed the adulterers by turning their genitals into carnivorous beasts, the people raised their fear of those who poisoned their gender by seeking revelry with their own kind or changing their body parts altogether – rejecting the beautiful design that God had given them. But after God melted the sexually alternate, the people of his parish still spoke with anxiety. They warned of those who banded together in opposition to those who praised and valued God's place in creation – those who foolishly worshipped imaginary gods or forsook the very idea of God altogether. Surely these people, who wore their ungratefulness a proudly as a scout's badge, were among the most sinister of all humankind.

Before long, the clouds were glowing red with the flames and blood of the burning bodies, the wind was thick with ash and the echoes of the screaming were bouncing between mountains and valleys. Yes, now the world was a perfect place – free of the horrors that stifled it from blooming. God smiled at the fires and laughed to the people, extending his arms to welcome their joy.

He felt a hand on his shoulder. He turned to see the man, Brian, at his back, looking out to the bloody landscape.

'You should come inside,' said Brian.

And God followed Brian up the uneven stone steps, past the priest who was running to embrace his people in rapt astonishment. Brian opened the heavy church doors and held them open to allow God into the shadowy church interior.

'I would like you to read this,' said Brian, holding out a large paperback tome. Its edges were ragged and yellowed and its spine struck with white furrows. 'It's a Bible. It's their account of your time here on Earth. From before.'

'From before? But however would they know about that?'

'Give it a read.'

And so God sat down at a pew under a curtain of cold light and flicked through the thousands of ghostly-thin pages of the heavy tome. His face remained impassive as he absorbed the ancient words. Brian watched him in silence until, after a few tense minutes, God reached the final pages and flipped the hard cover onto the flat body of the Bible.

God rapped his fingers on the back of the tome before standing and approaching Brian at the centre of the church aisle. Wrapping Brian in a tight embrace, God pulled Brian's face to his chest and whispered to him.

'You say this book holds the words of the holy men who speak of me. It holds the birth and death of humankind in a strange and wonderful poetry. You struggle to define yourselves, you people – you called on me when I was absent and impregnated all that you saw with my will and motive. With me as your chaperone you raised cities, forged countries and organised yourselves in such an abstract and conflicted manner.'

Brian felt the air grow hotter but he could not see from their embrace; his blinded perspective brightened through his eyelids. God continued:

'Through such a strange reasoning, you have grown to embrace your own destruction: you foretold my arrival and wished me to rain fire upon all of the Earth. You yearned for it. You hated each other. Is this what you truly want, as a people? I gave you no rules or society, but you have learned to covet such violence - often in my name. Though it is truly fascinating, I find it far too unsavoury for my delicate palate.'

God released Brian from his grip and sighed. Something felt different; it was deathly quiet. Stroking Brian's cheek with a rough thumb, God twisted a resigned face. 'Let's start again,' he said.

Walking to the church doors, God looked back to Brian and told him not to worry and as the doors opened, Brian was momentarily muted by the change in scenery. As they walked out of the church, they were surrounded by a dense, towering garden with colours that crept between the trees and across the grass where young rabbits lopped between lanky mushrooms and lions dozed, curled up in the sun with happily snoozing deer. The town was gone.

'The people...?' asked Brian.

'No more people, Brian,' said God. 'I've decided that I don't care for people very much. A *person*? Now, that I like, Brian. I like you very much, and so I give you this. I was entranced by the ideas expressed at the beginning of your book – before it all became awfully uncivilised by those parasitic *people*. It's yours to roam in, Brian. Have fun with it, and I'll return in an aeon or so to catch up. I have abolished death, so you needn't be afraid.'

Brian looked around. 'But no people?'

'You don't need people, Brian. People are a very bad thing,' said God, standing taller than ever. 'But I'll let you in on a little secret. Somewhere in this garden – this planet encompassing garden – there is a very special woman, just for you.'

'A woman?'

'Just for you, my human friend.'

'But I'm gay.'

'Brain, you do complain an awful lot. I thought you were someone different. I've provided a whole world for you and your animal friends that I thought you'd love.'

'But you didn't ask–'

'Let's just see how you get along, and if you're still unhappy, we can talk about it when I return. That's compromise. Now, I must be getting on – you really don't want to see how long my to-do list is. I still have to iron out the kinks in quantum mechanics – there is still far too much left to interpretation there.'

And God scratched his beard, turned in the air, and was gone.

Brian began to walk between the trees. He wondered if he should strip to the skin, now he was alone, but wherever he turned the penetrating gaze of the fauna followed him, so he decided to keep his clothes on for the time being and see how the centuries fared. He found a glade in the shadow of a family of elms and lay down among the fallen leaves. Then he slept.

Matthew's Spectre

Matthew and Gilda Boleyn had been married for as long as they could love. Now their hair was brushed silver and their skin coarsened by time's gentle fingers, though their bodies remained strong and their minds sharp. In their younger years, they had both gorged themselves on books and schooling, their time spent exploring the twisting halls of academia, researching and experimenting in the hope of expanding humanities horizons. They had fallen in love many decades ago, sharing their fascinations over nibbles at a university soiree. From that night forward they were pained by separation. The love they shared was the only real love that either of them would ever know. But this is not a tale of love.

Matthew was distinctly stern of character. A bulging vein climbed his temple, forever impressing a frown from his forehead. He was short in stature and in tone, thunderous upon all who chose to criticise his ideas on a whim. This is not to suggest that he lacked kindness, warmth and compassion; his heart was simply more lion than lamb.

Dear, sweet Gilda preferred to keep her fire at arm's length. She was gentle with the ignorant and patient with their anger; she gave them a horizon of time to unleash their indignation before calmly walking them back through their bluster. With a kindly smile, she would knock down their feeble assertions, one by one, like drunken sailors at stormy seas. But she and Matthew shared the same goal – to bring an understanding of how to walk closer to the truth with the right way of thinking.

They had little need for money these days. Between them, they had accumulated a comfortable wealth thanks to the surprising popularity of their academic books and observational diaries. In their later years, they gathered their wealth, packed up their bags and travelled to all the impoverished corners of the world to help educate the struggling masses.

For years they journeyed together across and between continents, meeting with children and adults alike. They spoke with the fire of their life's work, fascinating their audience with photography and tools, charts and drawings, journals and fact bites, speaking to groups as small as an ensemble and as large as a multitude – and always for free. But Matthew and Gilda came not just to bestow the collected knowledge of the world, but to share how such knowledge came to be known. Why were they confident about the atom and not the unicorn? Each photograph, each little artefact and every piece of truth about the world came with the stories of the people who came to understand them. These were the tales they came to tell.

They would tell the children: when it comes to matters of fact, the feelings in your heart may lead you astray. Be sure to rendezvous with your head before leaping ahead. The greater your dilemma, they would say, the greater the need for certainty.

One particular summer, they trekked to a rural village which sat beside a dusty plain of stiff grass at the slight bend of a stream. The village was a beautiful red colour, the sun-baked wooden homes sitting among the hot yellow earth and flora. The people there were a tribe rich in society and agriculture, but simple in resource. As the Boleyns arrived, the mothers held the heads of their children at their hips as the elder men drew forward to meet them. Their greeting was a staccato fire of interrogation armed with fear that the Boleyns had come to bewitch the village youth with dangerous ideas from beyond the mountains.

'Where do you come from?'

'What do you want?'

'Why are you here?'

Gilda, in her gentle voice tones, assured the men of their benevolence, 'We bring stories and studies and sensibility. We bring no violence; only a knowledge to share. We wish for nothing from in return but kindness and peace.'

But the village men were not interested in Gilda's words. They appeared somewhat spooked that she spoken at all; they twitched from her like a horse with flies on its eyes. They turned their focus to Matthew who spoke no differently than Gilda; he assured them that they only wished to expand their minds and hearts with the knowledge they had long spent accumulating. He tapped his head and his chest with two fingers as his spoke, his eyes unblinking. The elders huddled in a fury of foreign whispers before, eventually, allowing the Boleyns to stay.

Mr Kingman was the leader of the elder village men. He was a tall, broad man with bare, thick arms. His chest was thistled with a diagonal thatch of pale white flesh: the lingering vestige of some terrible burn, Glenda guessed. He did not look particularly old – barely into middle age – but he stood with a heavy charge across his shoulders. He was proud of his village and wary of 'poisonous infection' from outsiders. He was quick to promise the Boleyns that he would be present at all of their teachings to make sure no wickedness was spilled from their lips. As he spoke, he beat a long iron farming tool into his palm.

'They will remember that they are guests here and no more,' Mr Kingman urged to the other elders. 'Though they come from a rich land, they must know that they are no more entitled.'

The following morning, after a stuttered sleep, Matt and Gilda spoke on open ground in the dry, footstep-worn area between the grassland and the village. They wanted the villagers to be able to come and hear them talk between the shifts of their daily work. All the while, Mr Kingman cast a long shadow over the Boleyns from the perimeter, tapping the sharpened end of his farm tool on the dirt in a tight, dotted ring around the lesson. Tap, tap, tap.

Matthew spoke to the people in a booming voice as he looked over their heads to the infinite sky beyond. How easy it was to imagine a multitude of fantastical ideas as to how it all came to be; how the pieces worked together like clockwork: never failing, always turning; how difficult to peer into the works and understand the mechanism.

'But it is not a terrible thing to be unsure,' he warned. 'Do not be swayed by spurious suggestions and inane ideas. Do not allow your mind to canter into the wild, where the faeries and the unicorns dwell, without good reason.'

Mr Kingman snorted and stamped his cane extra hard. Dust and stone kicked into the air and he spat at the ground.

Gilda sat the children down by the cool air of the lake and asked them how many different creatures they thought lived in the surrounding lands.

'Two!' shouted a boy. 'No, three!' he added as a cricket hopped to his knee.

'Six!' yelled a girl.

'Seventeen!' another suggested.

The youth of the village were kept close to the boundaries and so were most unaccustomed to the hunting and exploring of the older folk.

'Why don't we explore for ourselves and see if any of your suggestions were right?' said Gilda.

So she led the children on an expedition. They scoured the grass and counted the creepy-crawlies; they lifted the soil to find the worms; they climbed the trees to see the birds; they paddled the river to see the fish. And still Gilda insisted there was much more life out there.

She showed them the claw-scraped holes of the burrowing animals, trotting footprints of hyena packs, broken carcasses in piled earth. She told them, 'You see, children – sometimes we know there are things out there by the clues they leave behind... even if we can't see them!'

One of the boys stepped forward. 'Like the beast that comes in the night?' he asked.

'Say again?' asked Gilda Boleyn.

'The beast that comes in the night,' said the boy. 'He comes to the village sometimes, always at night. He steals the girls away. They say if we don't let him, he'll burn our village away with fire.'

'Well,' said Gilda, swallowing a tremor, 'how do you know he exists, this night beast?'

'Because that's what they told us,' said the boy. 'Mr Kingman, all the elders and everybody. Why else would the girls never come back?'

'You may be right, little one,' said Gilda, bringing her voice to a hush. 'But I tell you children – and this is important, now – you make sure you check for evidence of the night beast, just like we did today. We saw tracks and dens and eggshells, did we not? Make sure you seek out the tell-tale signs of the beast so you can be sure he's really out there.' And Gilda ruffled the boy's hair and gave him a pair of binoculars to play with.

For the next few lessons, Mr Kingman declined to supervise. Gilda and Matthew weren't sure where he'd disappeared to but they were certainly glad for the breathing space. They took it in turns to let the people and children experiment and play with their shiny equipment without Mr Kingman's bulging gaze hovering at their periphery.

But Mr Kingman soon returned and, with him, was a group of large men, their muscles bulging like twisted balloons, their irises swallowed by the whites of their eyes. They pointed at Gilda, shouting, 'Witch! A Witch!' Gilda protested and held up her arms, but they beat her wrist down with their clubs. The children watched, frozen silent until the women hurried them to their homes.

Mr Kingman and the men dragged Gilda and Matthew through the dirt and across the stones, far away from the village and into the wilderness. The sharp stones in the ground jabbed into them and shook their bones as they were pulled ever farther. Eventually they were thrown to the ground and rolled like rag dolls under the sun. The men snarled. And they spat on them and stamped and kicked them purple. They took out large blades and lifted them high so they caught the sun like fire. And they brought them upon Gilda again and again until she was silent and fought no more. Matthew lay winded and drained, half-turned onto his belly, staring into her empty eyes, curtained with blood.

The men looted their pockets and stole away, their voices disappearing in the distance until the wind in the grass dominated the ambiance. Matthew kept his eyes locked on Gilda's as the strength returned to his body and he was able to take her broken body in his arms and hold her, shaking and weeping as the stars filled the sky, the phlegm choked his throat and the salt burned his face.

When he was finally able to release her and look out into the darkness, he knew they were utterly lost. He dug into the earth until his fingers bled and gently laid Gilda inside. He drew his face to hers and realised that nothing he could say to her would be enough, so he kissed her cheek and slept beside her for the last time in the cold dark wilderness.

The next morning, Matthew took a last glance back to the turned earth and began to walk out into the world, hoping to find a path home.

The terrain was vicious. The sun threw down its heat in unending cascades as the wind drew dryness into his lungs and the landscape plunged in empty homogeny towards the horizon. Knowing he would not last long without it, Matthew spent the first day searching for water, his body empty and desiccated from a long day of unquenched thirst. By following the busy tracks of thirsty wildlife he was able to find a narrow, bending stream by the eve of the day. The following day he wound a long path, avoiding mountains and deserts, trying to keep the river in sight as his thirst burned into him. By nightfall on the third day, he was unsure how far he had travelled but drew hope, knowing that all rivers must end, and that settlers are drawn to build towns within reach of water.

He was looking over the blue, moonlit grasslands from a rocky rise, when he was disturbed by unnatural shadows that shifted and rose around him, lifting from the cracks and crevices into a tall, unsettled, human-like form. The cumulus, faceless stranger glided over the stone towards him, bending and turning as though to appreciate the view.

'You've lost your way, Matthew,' said the Spectre.

Matthew stared at the Spectre, frozen, his cracked lips tightly shut. Beneath the mist of the Spectre's visage whirled the shadow of a thousand buried faces, looking out in agony – screaming perhaps. Or was his mind playing tricks with the noise of the ever-shifting shape? The Spectre waiting patiently, staring quietly, just a few paces from him. Matthew slowly allowed an unbroken flow of air to his lungs.

'I've lost far more than my way,' he said, at last, his lips pursing.

The Spectre extended a hand to his shoulder, but Matthew twisted away, for he knew the Spectre to be an illusion, projected by his loneliness.

'Begone, Spectre!' he shouted. And the Spectre disappeared into the air. He was alone again.

The next day, Matthew lost sight of the river for a while as he tried to hasten his journey by cutting a straight over the land. He had grown worried about his madness and needed to escape this wild void as soon as possible. But, when he noticed the earth was parched and broken underfoot he began to panic and cry out for help. No one appeared. Even the wind was silent, and the clouds themselves seemed to have abandoned him. He cried out further and this time heard a voice, thick in the dead air, saying:

'Again, I find you lost, Matthew.'

The Spectre stood tall, rippling in the heat like a mirage, black against the bright noon.

'Begone, Spectre!' said Matthew, from his knees.

'But, of course,' said the Spectre, with what amounted to a bow. 'You should know, however, that water is to the east,' And he was gone again, in a twist of disturbed smoke.

Matthew surveyed all directions. Would he have walked east of his own accord? He suspected he would have, so took the Spectre's hint, but for his own reasons. Definitely for his own reasons.

After an hour's walk, he found the river again and knelt to sip from its clear, turning waters. He looked down into the eyes of his frenzied reflection, the pebbled bed rippling through his skin.

'I'll never stray from you again,' he whispered.

He slept the night within range of the sounds of the chattering water. It comforted him. He dreamt of Gilda – at first her laughter made him euphoric but then it exploded into her slaughter and shook him awake. As the sunlight broke through his adjusting eyes, he saw that soup of smoky colour in the dirt beside him. Its curling edges licked at his side.

'She won't cloud your dreams forever,' said the Spectre.

'What do you know of my dreams?' whispered Matthew.

The Spectre turned, 'You call out in your sleep.'

'You're not real!' said Matthew. 'I've read the books, Spectre. I've seen the histories and the hunts. There are no ghosts or ghouls, demons or devils. No trace, no evidence, no verified sighting. You are a part of my mind and nothing more!'

'And here, you speak to me now, with confidence, like a brother.'

'Who else do I have, Spectre.'

And so, surrendering to his loneliness, Matthew allowed the Spectre to accompany him on his search for civilisation. The Spectre lent him guidance on direction but Matthew resisted, preferring to make his own decisions, for he knew the Spectre had no more knowledge than he. He was only homo, not sapient.

'But how are your decisions any better than mine?' the Spectre noted. 'Yesterday, you led yourself to despair and only after you took my heed did you find a way back to water.'

Matthew grunted. He was in no mood to debate with an apparition. He still preferred to be in control of his own path and that was that. But by the afternoon, Matthew stood in the cool of the Spectre's shadow, his blistered skin relieved by the shade. He spoke to the Spectre about Gilda. They chatted about how they had met when she'd helped chase down his old hat that had been stolen by the wind; how he'd convinced her to court him under the rail sheltered arch of the library porch; how they had made a life together in their squat little brick house across from the railway station. He laughed at his own anecdotes with an echoing distance, speaking as though about a person long-lost in history with an old school friend.

'And then you decided to teach together, all over the world,' said the Spectre.

'Yes, to show people not to fear superstition. To free them, and allow them to see the world as it really is.'

'I know, but why? Why would you do that?'

'A lot of people see their lives through a distorted fog, Spectre. We saw ourselves as opticians for the mind, shaping the lens for thought so that people could make open-eyed decisions without myopic misconceptions.'

'But you also teach the very poor and the wretched. Perhaps the idea of a better world –within their own and beyond – gives them comfort in their hardship. Why would you so cruelly steal that idea away?'

'Don't think that I haven't considered that, Spectre. But a better world does exist. Gilda and I came from that world: of schools and wealth and comfort. And that place grew from a past as meagre as this. These people will struggle to catch up if they wait for spirits and hocus pokery.'

Matthew walked tall as the Spectre pondered his world, its body curled dark fumes around him. The sun had fallen below the horizon and sky was inked in purple.

'And how can you be sure there is one truth, or that we all see the same parts of that truth?' said the Spectre.

'I can't be certain of anything, but as long as all the evidence points to a single reality, shared by us all, then that's the world I'll believe in. No hidden sorcery, no angry gods.'

'So tell me, Matthew,' said the Spectre, 'what do you make of me?'

Matthew looked into the Spectre's fogged facade and said, 'Some delusions can bring comfort. But they will not lead me true.'

Matthew's already fragile sleep was fractured as the Spectre continued to prod him with questions about reality and perception into the night. The next day was cooler, but Matthew was weary. His mind aching from stress and sorrow, it was easier to gamble on the Spectre's ability to direct him. They turned east in silence and headed up a steep, rocky slope together. Before long, they were high enough for Matthew to look back over his previous day's path. The spectacle didn't prick his awe as it might if he could have shared it with Gilda.

'How far until we reach the water again?' Matthew asked.

'You're asking me, I notice,' said the Spectre.

'Yes, please just tell me how far.' Matthew spoke in a dry, gravelly tone, unable to hide his exhaustion. Even keeping his focus was becoming depressingly laborious.

'What if I told you it was another two miles,' said the Spectre.

'Good,' said Matthew. 'I can probably walk that far before I need to rest again.'

'But what if I said it was ten miles? Or twenty?' The Spectre tiled its head to him until its whole body began to spiral and coil, cycling in and out of its human shape.

Matthew's face was flushed with fear – not at the Spectre, but at himself. 'Say nothing more.'

'But why not, Matthew?' said the Spectre, turning and twisting.

'Go away!' said Matthew, shielding his eyes. 'Begone! Begone!'

'But why, Matthew?'

Matthew did not look at the Spectre and kept his head down as he hopped across the uneven rocks, trying to continue on.

'But, Matthew...'

'I can do two things, Spectre,' said Matthew. 'I can believe you exist, or I can not.'

'Indeed, those are your only choices, Matthew. But which to choose?'

'How? How can I believe you are real, when I have no good reason to?'

'Your eyes have me in good authority.'

'Eyes are so easily deceived!' said Matthew. 'Why, I tell people every day that the aliens and ghosts and angels they swear they saw were never there. And now here we are, talking to one another, leading one another. Where does it end? What are you?' Matthew's throat broke. 'I don't want to be alone.'

'Calm yourself. You are not alone. If you just relax your prickly inhibitions a little and allow me to lead you home, you can leave this desolation.' said the Spectre.

'Not if you're not real. If you're not real then you might well be a worse gamble than trusting my own instincts.'

'But if you don't believe in me, then you are happily accepting your own madness. And if you are mad, then who are you to trust your own instincts?'

'How can I trust a mind so broken and fragile as to have conjured you?'

'You followed me this far, Matthew. You've spent a very long time reserving your trust and scowling at wondrous things with your sceptical eyebrow. Allow yourself a moment of peace.'

The path dropped steeply at its edge. Matthew saw the fast, high air flick the vaporous edges of the Spectre, whose dark gaze followed his eyes.

'I don't want my mind to be broken, Spectre,' said Matthew. 'My mind is all I have. I have no wife. My riches and possessions are just flourishes of an empty life. What am I now if I cannot tell fantasy from reality? If you were true, I'd be content in my sanity.'

'And you'd have ventured out beyond the threshold of the world you thought you knew.'

'I suppose.'

'What do you want, Matthew?'

'I...' Matthew croaked. The wind whipped his tears sideways. 'I just want Gilda back.'

'Exactly. In all your walking and searching, that's all you've ever wanted. And you can have it. I've come to take you home. I've seen the other side where your wife waits with patience. That's where you home is now. You can be together.'

'You know this?'

'All you have to do is jump.'

Matthew looked over his shoulder, where the Spectre gestured, back to the edge of the path where the Spectre's cloak flowed like heavy fluid over the falling stone face, where the wind kissed the void.

'She's just across the way, waiting.'

The edge was only a few feet away, the fall no further than a moment of bravery.

'Stop this nonsense,' said Matthew. His eyelids were puffed red, his eyes glassy.

'You let me bring you up here, in trust. You want it to be true. You need it to be true.'

'I do! I wish she were just across the way, as you say.' Matthew greedily eyed the disappearing stone edge. 'Oh, I wish I could just step out to meet her. But wishing cannot force a falsehood.'

'What else do you have? Stay here, alone in the middle of nothing?'

'There is no option. I cannot choose what is real and what isn't.'

And Matthew fell to his knees and sobbed. He looked over the cliff edge and saw nothing more than the blur of death. He cried out to the wind and heard no response. When he rose, the Spectre was gone. And he lay until his exhaustion pulled him to sleep.

His sleep was quiet and dreamless. He awoke under the curl of the moon, and descended the path alone. He dusted the grit from his cheeks. The night was clear and he followed the long blue shadows, consigned to facing the world in all its difficulties.

The horizon stretched out long beyond his familiarity but he was confident that he could walk beyond its edges and, one foot at a time, make his way home.

On a Hypotenuse

Olly met Clyde on a hypotenuse,
The nature of which had poor Clyde most confused,
'This shape has three sides,
'Dearest Olly', said Clyde,
'But all angles are right and that just can't be true!'

'You must be mistaken,' was wise Olly's song,
'This cannot be a three-sided polygon,
'If all angles are ninety,
'And you measured precisely,
'It's surely rectang'lar, or something's gone wrong!'

'Then walk round, dear Olly, you'll have to declare,
'The first corner turns like the point of a square,
'Two more turns, the same,
'And a short walk again.
'And we're back where we started – oh, how I despair!'

Then in Olly's great mind, an idea became clear,
'It spans half the world!' he declared with a cheer
Oh Clyde, we've been stupid,
'Fixated by Euclid,
'This shape isn't flat, but on our Earthly sphere!'

Supernature

A long time back, quite suddenly and unexpectedly, the quiet of Canopy Woods was shaken by a long and mysterious shriek. It was a shriek that echoed throughout the woods, shattering the birds from the trees and forcing the mammals from their burrows. Time and again, the scream froze the air and the fauna pointed in panic. The animals gathered among their own kind, turning to their elders for answers: what was this almighty din and whatever did it mean?

The foxes pulled flat to the floor, their black ears pricked and turning in a jitter from their fierce, fiery heads. In their cowed respect of nature, they believed that it was the voice of the forest itself, scolding them for leaving their dens during the day, when they were supposed to hunt their prey at night. The elder foxes, with pale eyes and skinny limbs, had long condemned these modern changes to the skulk, baring their teeth as the youngsters walked and hunted in the daylight. This, they argued, was not the way of the fox; the forest was warning them to keep to their night hours. After all, the screams only came by day.

The new generation of vixens who encouraged the hunting of daytime voles and rabbits were chastised and shamed: their ragged ears the scars of their punishment. From then on, young vixen kits habitually had their ears scratched in twain to mirror the shame of those who had gone before them; a reminder to the skulk of how to live their lives with respect and propriety.

The hawks saw things differently. They had not panicked. Instead, they waited and tried to understand something about the shriek. They held their sculpted beaks high as they perched a cool grip on the branches of an old ash tree. The brightest among the hawks of the time was a sleek bird named

Stephen. His eyes flashed black with constant thought as he perched on the highest branch. He did not crane his neck to address the others, though he stretched his impressive wingspan into the sunlight as he words hit their fervour. He noticed that the shriek rang out during hunts – his mind turned to a poor young hawk found with his feathers dirty and ruffled around his belly. He had recently died soon after a successful catch, without warning or expectation. Stephen reasoned that the scream was likely a warning that the prey was poisonous and not to be touched. He recalled the bright toads that warned of their deadliness with their skin of alarming colours. This, he posited with his talons tightening their grip on his branch, was something similar, only with the alarm of sound and not colour! The hawks all dipped their beaks with agreement – if they heard the warning sound while on the hunt, they would abandon their prey and find a new kill. It was the safest way to live.

Down among the bracken and the crisp, dead leaves, however, the voles were rejoicing. Small, brown pudgy bodies were circling through the grass with excitement, occasionally pausing to nibble a seed and stare into the thick of the woods with their bright, black eyes. Legend had spoken of the promise made by the ancient and revered founding vole, Anton, whose spirit would always keep watch over the vole herd and assure its safety. They knew the scream to be Anton's as surely as if he had appeared before them to sound it. He was scaring away their predators, fulfilling his prophecy to keep his beloved descendants safe. Why else would the biting foxes shy from the sunshine and the screeching hawks turn and flee?

And so the voles strutted smartly about the forests, their ears loose and their noses wiggling high. The other creatures were an inferior kind, skulking in envy, so the voles claimed the forest for voledom, danger be damned! There was to be no more scattering to the darkness for them!

Generations later, in the daily blood-stained light of dusk, the foxes would brace and scrabble at the edges of their dens, waiting for the sky to darken and the screams to rest. Some, after a night's hunting, would stay out to catch the first warmth of dawn; others stuck tightly to their code, not letting a drop of sunshine touch them. These orthodox foxes frowned upon the dawn stragglers for, although they knew that the forest would let them hunt until the first cry of the morning, hunting by sunlight was disrespectful and frown-worthy in the extreme.

Summer was the dreaded season. Long hours of light kept the foxes locked underground for far longer that they liked, and the risk of fights breaking out was high. The young foxes itched to leave the suffocating dens but the elders feared the retaliation of the forest and viciously punished any who attempted to break the curfew. Rules were laid down. Uncrossable guidelines, to which every fox must adhere: those caught out of after first light would be kept from hunting for the following night; any foxes attempting to escape the skulk to form a new society would be punished by death.

Violence was rife: if a fight broke underground, the claustrophobia heightened the already inevitable risk of injuries, sometimes leading to an unfortunate death. Bitter, sniping arguments between the elders and the youth could last the length of the day, often resulting in torn tails and ears while angry blasphemy towards the forest for keeping them underground was punished by frenzied mauling. The once silky-red fur of the proud, flighty foxes had become matted, scratched and dirty. But the elders feared the forest. Control of the skulk was vital for its own survival, so the elders had no choice but to heap authority upon them. Drooling for an ounce of power and responsibility, the maligned youth yearned for their graduation to elder status. As generations passed, every new wave of the elder council grew more muscular in its drive. The imbalance in the skulk grew so large that any power became desperately sought – not for responsibility, but for the sake of power itself.

Meanwhile, the hawks continued to pass their knowledge of the shriek down their bloodlines. The wariness of the terrible warning cry grew to a nervous mania. Some hawks grew so hungry that they would sometimes ignore the warning shriek and just eat a little illegitimately caught prey. Just a little nibble, they'd promise, with a hopeful gamble. Some of these impatient hawks were lucky, but others died within a few days or weeks of the risky meal; many more suffered dizziness and pain for long periods after. The unlucky served as a warning to the others, who were only glad for it. There was no escaping the fact that there was something toxic in the fauna.

But the hawks, in their skinny dizziness, knew that they were doing right, as they had been rewarded for rigorously fighting through the hunger and sticking to the method. They had noticed they if they obeyed, voles started to present themselves as meals. It was the most absurd sight: fat, juicy voles walking plainly into the open of the forest, without fuss or fear; some even dancing or stretching out lazily on their backs. It seemed that, if one observed the warnings, there were benefits to be had as the forest rebalanced the circle of life and brought them rewards.

Unfortunately, it was hard to know when, or if, these gift voles would appear. Some hawks would find themselves near starvation between meals, waiting for their gifts. Life was hard, especially when the screams became ever more frequent: the poison was spreading. Voles, rats, tits and sparrows – all became potential carriers of the disease. But the hawks were sure to end each night by reminding each other how thankful they were that they had been able to recognise the warnings at all.

Ultimately, the cast of hawks met to deliberate their future. Their presence in the forest seemed doomed to extinction. They decided to abandon the forest and set exodus for a new ecology. They would seek out a land without disease, where they could hunt with freedom and dignity like the hawks of old. Yes, that seemed like a fine plan. The word spread.

Life continued to blossom for the herd of voles who swaggered about the forest like red-breasted robins. Protected by the Great Anton, they were free to eat and play and mate as they wished. The foxes stayed hidden underground, hardly ever to be seen, and the hawks turned and fled at Anton's call. It seemed clear that the sacred culture that the voles had developed and polished had won them great favour from Anton as he watched over them. Still, there remained some transgressions in the herd...

Occasionally a vole would be all alone, out on the forest floor – maybe dancing between the bluebells or supping the dew from low leaves – when a hawk or fox would verily snatch him or her away! For the snatched vole, this was the ultimate shame. If the Great Anton refused to defend you from attack, you were truly unworthy of voledom. The families and friends of a fallen vole were allowed a single day of mourning before the deceased became an unmentionable.

Some wondered if it was foolish for the voles to walk among predators so casually. But the hunters really did seem so hesitant to approach, and so disinclined to kill, that living under Anton's protection truly must be the wisest and happiest choice.

One day, with dawn illuminating Canopy Wood, the foxes were on the return from a night's hunt when they noticed the hawks casting a shadow over the foliage. It was unusual to see so many of them gathered at once and so the foxes cried out to them: 'What are you doing, Hawks?'

'The forest is awash with poison, Foxes. Surely, you too have noticed?'

'No, Hawks. All is well with the woods.'

'Your kind has not suffered from the kill, Foxes?'

'Not at all. And your kind still hunts by day, I see.'

'Of course, Foxes.'

How unfair, they both declared. But at that moment, an owl hooted from a higher branch.

'Foxes, Hawks. I couldn't help by overhear, what with my dish-shaped face and all. What put such fanciful ideas of poison and sunlight prohibition into you heads?'

'The shriek!' cried the foxes and the hawks.

'The shriek is the command of the forest,' said the foxes.

'Nay! 'Tis a warning of toxic prey,' said the hawks.

The owl ruffled his feathers and cocked his head. 'You are all quite mad! That is not what the shriek is.'

The foxes and the hawks looked to one another with bemusement. What made owls such experts on the shriek?

'The legend of the shriek is far more interesting than your strange ideas, my friends!' The owl cocked his round head and stretched his wings. 'For you see, when my ancestors first heard the shriek, they, like you, had no idea what it could be. No one had heard such a thing. But they were determined to find out. So they began a journey to follow the sound, tracing it out of the forest and across the land... and do you know what it was? Humans!'

The foxes and hawks collapsed to laughter. Humans had never made such a noise!

'Indeed not. Not before then, anyhow. But one must never underestimate the human. They seek to be like the birds and have built themselves great machines in which they take to the skies. The machines rest not too far from here and, as they fly over these woods, they scream like the devil. Terribly graceless, lumbering machines they are – unworthy to share our skies, of course.'

'Naturally, we couldn't believe it at first but oh, we made sure. We watched the skies for days and sure enough, every scream followed a flying machine.'

Humans flying in the sky? And the owls were supposed to be intelligent! The hawks and foxes scoffed and jeered 'til the owl snapped his beak, turned and flew. They told their kind the owl's story – the foxes called them 'dangerous buzzards' and the hawks declared that they had 'fallen from excellence to become nothing more than feathered clowns'. The owls cared little for the opinions of other animals and flew high under a darkening sky as an almighty scream erupted from the giant air machine with blinking wings.

The hawks left the woods and the foxes continued to keep out of the light. And, as the airport expanded and the screams grew ever more frequent, the foxes grew fearful and the voles ever bolder. And the owls, with a wry turn of the beak at the eccentricity of their neighbours, plucked the willing bounty from the land – the vole, the rabbit and the rat – with only the slightest resistance or competition. The foxes watched sullenly from their dens as those villainous owls debased the forest, their stupidity keeping them from propriety. Oh, how the day would come when the forest would swallow them up without mercy or burn them from their nests!

And the skinny, angry foxes laughed at the owls.

And the dancing, daring voles laughed at the foxes.

And the fat, happy owls laughed at the voles.

And the world turned, indifferently.

The Dream Machine

As it was every day, Derek awoke sideways. His body was wrapped in the thin, flowery duvet; his head buried in his two, cold, flattened pillows. He stared at the dry, greasy smudge that stared right back at him every morning like a ghostly eye from the very centre of the window where the curtains didn't quite meet. He made a mental note, as he did every time he woke, to buff the window clean.

'Are you going to turn that off?'

His wife kicked at his legs from across the bed, her voice reaching a crescendo on the final word.

Derek's thoughts about the window smudge had inflated inside his head and blocked his ears to the alarm clock that trilled from across the room. Slumping heavily out of the cosy bed, he let the cold air pinch at his naked body and turned the alarm off. Another new day.

He showered for a little too long. The shower was a warm and wonderful intermission from the fierceness of reality and he feasted on those precious few minutes of isolation, staring dreamily at the water curling around his toes and into the drain through the trapped hair. But the moment was all-too-quickly broken by the impatient banging on the bathroom door.

Time dropped out from beneath him and he suddenly found himself dressed and late for work. With his last tear of toast flopping lazily from his mouth, he mumbled something about trains, abandoned his cold, filmy tea and grabbed his bag. His wife, Angela sat to his right, applying colour to her face by a tiny, gold hand mirror. He pecked her a goodbye kiss; their eyes were too busy to meet. As Derek left his street, he wondered if he had even seen his wife's face that morning, whether he'd have even noticed if that woman in his house has been replaced by an imposter. He dropped his eyes to the damp-patched pavement, his face curling into an unconscious snarl and frightening a little girl who was out walking her dog.

Derek walked downhill past the tall, iron streetlamps, their honeyed gaze already cowed in submission to the morning's blue light. Waiting ahead in a lazy fog was the station – the gateway that would lead him and hundreds of other suited folks out to the city. He took his daily position on the smoke-stained platform between the man flicking idly through a newspaper and the woman with who always wore corsets so tight that he often wondered where she kept her organs. The third carriage would pull up alongside them here. He'd sit in his seat, facing forward and wait for her to embark at the next station along.

*

'Who is that, at the other end of the carriage?' Angela pushed her finger into the screen, blurring a soft streak over the glass. She clenched Derek's shoulder as he lay asleep in their marital bed. Dreadlocks of coiled copper wires cascaded from his scalp and into the great, brass machine parked clumsily at the foot of the bed.

'Who do you mean?' said the doctor to Angela.

'There's a blonde woman who just got on the train. There: the fat one in the purple dress. The one who smiled at him, at my Derek.'

'This is your husband's life. I'm afraid I don't know who any of these people are.'

'Why is she smiling at him?' Angela said, her words peaking at a desperate pitch. She rolled her head toward Derek, her eyebrows raised to her hairline, as though he would answer. But Derek was asleep; he merely sniffed and flickered his eyelids a little. Angela turned back to the doctor, her expression so stern that her eyes and mouth had drawn right into her nose, creating an island of ferocity at the centre of her face. 'You say you can control these people? Including the purple woman?'

'Of course.'

'Make her talk to him.'

*

Derek watched her step onto the train – carefully, as always, so she didn't trip in her tall heels. She was wearing that purple dress. They exchanged smiles, as had become their strange tradition and he waited for her to dissolve into her book, at which point he would let his eyes drift to the window and watch the world pass by. The familiar landmarks would guide him into town: the iron-gated park, the cold neon high street, the brick-and-iron shell of a long-abandoned factory. He'd flick the occasional glance her way, just to see if they might share a second moment, but they never did. He always lost out to that book.

But today, she didn't open her book. She held his gaze and smiled. Apparently changing her mind about her usual seat, she sashayed past the bulky bags and chubby bottoms that blocked the aisle and settled into the empty seat next to Derek. His throat tightened.

'Hello,' she said.

*

'We have a choice. We can give her every word and every move and puppet her like a marionette,' said the doctor, 'or we can just leave it to play out as his own mind sees fit.'

'Oh, you must let him do it,' Angela said. Pulling in closer to the screen, she released her grip on her sleeping husband's shoulder, leaving white nail-streaks in his skin. 'I asked to see into his head, didn't I?'

*

'Hello,' said Derek.

She smiled at him. He smiled back. The silence grew. How pathetic – he could think of nothing to say. What was there to say? He knew nothing about her.

'No book today?' he asked, shifting around in his seat.

'Oh. Yes, I have my book,' she said, her smile fading. 'I'm sorry, perhaps I've misunderstood...'

She gathered her things clumsily – her momentary lack of grace, a beautiful imperfection - and trotted away, her hair shimmering behind her.

*

'She left?' Angela stared at the screen, shocked. 'Bring her back, doctor. How am I supposed to learn anything from this? Oh Derek, in your own dream, as well...'

*

She turned on her heel and fell back into the seat next to him. She was laughing. 'Only joking! I knew what you meant!'

Derek laughed, though his face was still bore the horror at her departure. He wondered if he looked maniacal.

'Every day we share a smile. Every day. Yet we never say hello. Isn't that bizarre? So here I am. Emily.'

*

'He's always liked the name Emily,' Angela said with a snarl.

'It's only his mind filling in the details,' the doctor said. 'He has to give her a name, so he chose Emily, subconsciously.'

'Yes, I know that.'

*

'I'm Derek.' He took her fingers and shook them just the once. It was as polite and restrained a gesture as he could imagine. 'Are you on the way to work?' What a dull question.

'I'm on my way from work,' she, Emily, said. 'I work night hours in a laboratory.'

'Is that so? That's fascinating.' He'd always had a passion for science, though he'd never grasped it himself.

Emily told him all about her work: the machines, the mysteries, the evidences for the terrible crimes she'd been asked to investigate. Derek was transfixed by it all. All the colours of the world around him had faded, leaving Emily shining and vivid.

*

Angela was lying back on the bed, her shoulders stuffed into the pillows, her eyes unfocussed. 'This is so dull. I'm almost embarrassed for him, charming a woman with talk of science.'

The doctor sniffed. 'You should be glad that he only seems interested in-'

'You should stoke the fire,' she said, sitting up. 'Tempt him. Just a little.'

*

'You know,' Emily said, looking up at him through razor sharp eyelashes, 'While I do work all night, I'm not necessarily tired now.' She kept her eyes on his and flashed the smile again. Derek's spine tingled as Emily adjusted herself slightly, her bare knee brushing his trousered one, her skirt riding up just a centimetre or two. She let her hand fall softly on his thigh. Then, she threaded her fingers into his.

'Is there any more to you than a smile, Derek?' she asked, quietly.

The city was growing large in the opposite train window. Emily caught his gaze and, with one finger, pulled his face around towards hers.

'That place gets to see you every single day. All I get is a smile. Today can be different. Those city folk will still be waiting tomorrow; your suit and tie will forgive you.'

*

'Are these your words?' said Angela.

'No, I'm just nudging her along,' said the doctor. 'It's best to let his head do the leg work – if you see what I mean. It makes it more believable - to him, at least'

'Very curious indeed,' Angela tutted.

*

Derek paused for a moment, looking at Emily's hand lying over his. He let her fingers fall through his and released a long-held breath. Everything was still as they sat, letting their fingers moved slowly together: tiny, unspoken caresses. When the train pulled to a stop, he let her lead him away.

They broke jauntily through strangely familiar streets. The roads were brick-cobbled and the apartments were tall, water-stained metal and concrete monsters. Everything felt slightly out of place, jumbled together somehow. Had he been here before? He couldn't tell. Emily led him to a blue door that was so deeply scratched that he could see the many layers of paint, right through to the dark wood beneath. She poked a code into a graffiti-tagged aluminium keypad. The door buzzed and she heaved the door open, leading him into a damp grey-bricked corridor that blinked with the pale struggles of a dying tube light.

*

'I hope he gets sick from the fungus in the walls,' said Angela. Her eyes were now red and puffy. 'Why can't he at least go somewhere nice to break my heart?'

The doctor grunted, his head resting in his palm. Angela flashed a scowl at the back of his head. She was paying him more than she could rightly afford; he could at least pretend to be interested.

*

Emily slung her bag into the corner of the nearly empty room and grabbed Derek by his belt loops. In the brief moment hence, he noticed the islands of bare plaster floating in the magnolia of the wall and the balled-up chocolate wrappers under the uneven, tea-ringed table. Emily dipped her head and tossed that smile at him as they sank down into the plump sofa. Finally, in the quiet dark room, their lips met and their clothes fell away.

*

Angela stomped around the bedroom in the small space between the dream machine's trolley and the pale pine wardrobe. She had taken the small wedding photo from her bedside table and was gripping it tightly by the stand, staring into the happy, naïve faces within.

'I never wanted to believe it,' she sobbed, sucking in salty tears with each hiccupping breath. 'I just don't understand.'

'Then perhaps I don't understand either,' the Doctor rested on his knuckles. 'What was all of this about, if not to see this?'

'You think I *wanted* to see this?'

'I'm just a man with a machine, but I thought, as we brought them together and "stoked the fire", that we were pushing them together.' The doctor pulled a red cord as the base of the machine to quieten the moans from within the dream. 'Weren't we trying to snare him?'

'And he took the bait,' said Angela. 'Too willingly! How easy was it to break his loyalty to me, really? The first woman we saw...'

She looked at him, asleep on the bed, oblivious to their intervention. She wanted to slap his serenely sleeping face.

'But would he have slept with her if we hadn't pushed for it and kept her coming back?' the doctor asked. 'I thought that's what we were doing. He didn't seem interested at first, he made her a scientist.'

'He loves scientists. He wishes he *was* one.'

'But we did invite him back to her home, through her.'

'And he went, didn't he? It is a dream, I know. But what if – in real life – some *slut* really does approach him in earnest? He won't even stop to think of me. Look at him.'

She glanced to the screen the screen. Emily's legs were pointing to the ceiling, her underwear hanging from her toes, swaying with a ragged rhythm.

*

They separated, panting softly. Derek reached to the floor for his shirt. Emily propped herself up on her elbow, her chest flushed. Her breasts flopped across her chest like leaky water balloons; the jagged stretch marks shone on her hips in the pale window light. The room seemed greyer, darker that it had been. The wallpaper was peeling at the joins, the tea-coloured walls peering out from beneath.

Derek dressed in a hurry. He wasn't sure why – he had already called in sick; he had nowhere else to be. He just knew that 'somewhere else' was the place to be. He tied his shoes and looked up at her, still lying bent on the sofa. She watched him placidly with a lazy curiosity; only her eyes moved, the rest of her was still. He brushed a kiss on her cheek and, like an idiot, shook her hand before shuffling backwards from the room, watching her ghostly, empty face as her eyes followed him .

Outside, the air was warm and humid and walking in it felt like molasses. It seemed to take him an age to return to the station. Every movement was a great effort. He nearly didn't make it onto the train: as the guard blew his whistle, Derek was still slowly forcing his way forward, as if walking in lead boots on the ocean floor.

*

Angela has sat for minutes in silence. Her irises blazed from between her raw red eyelids. She finally broke the quiet. 'Why is he walking like an astronaut?' It was strangely infuriating - the nerve of him to walk to improperly!

'It's difficult to say,' said the doctor. 'Dreams can break the rules and if your mind is in a funny place, it can make the world a little stranger. He'd probably dealing with the fact that he's done something... unusual.'

'It had better be unusual.' she sniffed.

*

Derek rested his head against the train window. It vibrated against his skull, blurring his vision. He imagined his brain swirling around his skull like rice pudding in a washing machine. He was hungry.

There was no one else in his carriage. He was alone. The house would be empty when he returned; he would have to wait all day for Angela to come back and fill it. He felt his stomach tighten when he thought of her returning home, as he did every day when he heard her keys in the lock. He thought of the evening hours he'd spend grinding through the tension of their marriage, tip-toeing through the simplest discussions in fear of a conversational landmine. But, today, being alone felt worse, somehow.

*

'He looks dead,' Angela said, leaning into the screen. He had that same listless slump from the morning train.

The doctor kept quiet. A sniff came from the bed. Angela looked over to see Derek's cheeks wet with tears, the skin a blotched red.

'Take them off,' she said to the doctor. 'All of the wires, take them off.'

'In the middle-?'

'And be quiet about it.'

The doctor hurried over Derek. His skilled hands pulled the sensors from under his hair, rolled the wires over his wrist and coiled them back into the machine with barely a sound. He wheeled the machine out of the room, wincing at the creaking joints as it rattled over the threshold.

'The bill will be in the post,' he whispered.

Angela nodded. Derek stirred slightly with a pathetic whisper. Angela slid out of her clothes, took his hand in hers and shuffled under the sheets spooning her body around his. His skin was hot where they met. She wondered how icy she felt to him. He curled tighter into her and murmured, 'Angela.'

She strengthened her embrace and nuzzled her chin into his neck. 'I'm here, Derek.'

Anthropomorph

Is the rain rattling softly through layers of leaves,
The weeping of God as he wretchedly grieves?
And the thunder and earthquakes that crack through the land,
Do they break from the anger of his fisted hand?

Is the icicle hanging above your front door,
Biding for someone to leap on and gore?
Did the virus inside you, you now know is flu,
Wait for the day of your job interview?

When your puppy looks up at you; quiet, wide-eyed,
Could it be melancholy she's feeling inside?
And the crow that just stares at you, silent and black,
What is it he's planning – some kind of attack?

The car that won't start, the lights that turn red,
Conspiring against you, or all in your head?
When you need the computer, it'll freeze like a statue,
You smack it to warn it, 'play nice or I'll cut you.'

We see the world watching us as we pass through,
We want it to touch us, embrace us, due to,
Its relationship with us, we need it and so,
We assume that it needs us as well – alas, no.

Mrs Lemon's Children

We begin at the top floor. Up within the concrete and glass tower, over the orange-blue night light of Grimoire City's bars, clubs and drink halls, Bekali Casus, her face flared with neon, stared down at the tapestry of life below. She was far too familiar with its weave.

Grimoire: capital city; home to the full chorus of humanity, all trying to hot-step their way from birth to death without losing more than they gained. Quite a task, as a population crescendo had plucked and harvested the power, jobs and food they desired to scarce and precious commodities. No money for the spending, no coal for the lighting and very few bosses willing to give their worn and greasy coins to any more workers. The hearts and tempers of the men and women who wanted more than the world could share beat a heavy rhythm.

Thump, thump, thump.

Everybody felt it.

Bekali was lucky to have drawn herself a living from the dry harvest and choking poverty. She was a Secret Finder, hired to scope and sleuth where the rich dared not travel: the very heart of the city. It was as honest a living as any, dip-diving among her contemporaries, familiar with – but never part of – the social machine that ground its gears through day and night.

She looked at her face reflected inside the polished window of the tower, overlying the bright, scattered salt of city lights. She saw no shame. Everybody needed cash. Her big, brown eyes stared back into her, almost daring her to blink first. Their gaze crossed her bouffant black hair and dropped down the length of the bell of her body. Her blue-nailed fingers rested lightly on her hips; her lace stockinged feet stuffed into her dirty plimsolls. Even at this height, the bright colours of the city caught her through the glass and framed her luminous.

The carpet was thicker than she was used to. It gave way beneath her as she rocked on her heels, its dark, repeating pattern of squares looked blurry and distorted in the long pile. Thick, wood-stained bookshelves, stacked with leather-bound tomes, lined the edges of the office and the room seemed to absorb almost all of the light from the single, hanging bulb.

'So, you call it your city, do ya?'a pebbled, brassy voice spoke.

'Yes, sir, my city. I know ev'ry crack, ev'ry step, ev'ry street,' Bekali said.

'Good. That's good,' the man spoke, chewing on a dead cigar. Mr Saaed was a man of government. He helped to ease the clockwork, no matter how heavy the gears. Tick, tick, tick. 'Then you'll have heard of Mrs Lemon?'

'Ain't familiar,' said Bekali, 'but there's plenty a million missuses out there – don't know 'em all by name.'

'You had best get to know them then, eh? We've been hearing plenty of talk about Mrs Lemon.' He stubbed out his cigar nub. 'They say she's breeding her way to the top; say her family's so big now that she's got a child in every business in Grimoire. No one knows who they are, of course. Might even overcome us all by stealth. Suddenly, we're under the rule of these 'Lemons'. Understand?'

'So what's she look like? Where's she found?'

'That's your business, Casus. Can you find her or not?'

Passing through the white-steamed alleys, Bekali took a step down to the Old Harlot Bar. She knew the newspaper hacks knocked back liquor down in the black quarter. The journalists were always a good place to dig; they always buried themselves deep in the dirt. Sure enough, the pepper-headed young hack, Muppasa, was hunched in the shadows, bent over a scrappy notebook. Bekali took a glass of ale and sat with him. She clonked the ale to the table with a slosh.

'Plottin' your next miserable 'eadline, are ya?' she asked.

Muppasa puffed his greasy fringe aside to catch her eye. 'Misery writes itself, darlin',' he said, 'All I do is give it the flavour that makes it worth tastin'.'

'Whatcha know about a woman named Lemon?' Bekali gulped down a frothful of ale.

'Can't say it rings a bell,' he said, watching a liquid bead slip over her chin. 'Why, what've you got?'

'They say she's got a finger in ev'ry pie, don't they?' said Bekali. 'Children in ev'ry post – even government, they say. She's poppin' sprogs to take over by secret, ain't she?'

'That's new to me, Casus,' said Muppasa, scrawling furiously over his pad. 'Lemon... I'll ask around, maybe.'

And Bekali spent the night waltzing bar to bar about the black quarter, 'til her breath was soured with ale and her fingertips blackened with pencil lead. She whispered in the ears of the all the rag writers, but each answered the same. No one had heard anything. Bekali curled her lip and flicked her puffed cheeks. She felt them holding back.

Night. Dawn. Day.

Every newspaper read the same from the wrapped stacked piles by the vendors' carts and the chipped frame of the headline sandwich boards. Black, bold text: 'Who are the Lemons?'; 'One Family's Plot to Take Over.' She grimaced, a tick plucking the corner of her red lips. They had been holding back. Why?

Twitch, twitch, twitch.

Bekali skipped to the gangland. She was careful to avoid stepping on the sharper rocks that poked from the dusty, unmade roads that ran between the loping iron fences that divided the turf. She hopped over the fallen telegraph pole that had been the victim of a car accident many months back; servicemen hadn't dared to enter this part of town, so the locals has strung the wires to a flagpole. By day, gangsters plodded the streets, kick-kicking the dust, one hand pulling a cigarette to and from their mouths. She wasn't afraid of them. She knew they enjoyed her visits; they liked to hear her glimpses from the other territories. She sidled up to Big Ohna – a fat wine peddler, his boots a slow clomp to the pitter of her plimsolls.

'You see the papers, big man? The Lemons?' she asked.

'Yup, I've seen 'em. Why – what d'ya know about it?'

'Was gonna ask you the same question, wasn' I?'

'Hm,' Ohna growled. 'Well, I sell to all kinds, you know that. People not too keen on the name-sharin' though. Business is quiet round here, as it should be' He scratched his stubble. Rough, rough, rough. 'Still, I wouldn't be surprised if I'd met 'em from time to time. Sounds like them Lemons are everywhere.'

'Give us a shout if you see one for real, won't you?'

'I might, if you show a little interest in my Merlot, here.'

Whoever these Lemons were, their names had been long diffused into the stew of Grimoire's people and places. How could she find them? She kept her eyes to the papers.

'Suspected Lemon Influence in Burger Merger,' read one.

She sucked on a milkshake as she read, but found no clues within. Slurp, slurp, bubbles. Of course, she was already sitting within the white-tiled walls of the disputed burger restaurant as she scanned the newspaper under the clean fluorescent light. Such was her job. When she'd picked through the bun, lettuce, burger, and tomato (tossing the pickle), she twirled behind the counter to the tiny cubic offices behind, and found the restauranteuse.

'So,' she said, sitting on the edge of the crowded office desk, jerking at her skirt to hide her psychedelic pants. 'I 'ear you're in business with them Lemons, are ya?'

The restauranteuese pushed her chewed nails though her thinning hair. The skin was sagging from her ageing expression as if her face no longer had the strength or the will to hold it up. She exhaled. 'That's what they tell me. But blowed if I know. Could be anyone, these Lemons.' A tut. 'But now people won't shake my hand and do a deal if they see Lemon in the mix and I'm too old to grit my teeth and deal harder.'

'So you never met 'em?'

'Dunno. Met a couple of suited money-types. One blond, one kinda dark. Neither called themselves Lemon though.' The restauranteuse rested her cradled hands together on the desk, between a stack of old invoices and an army of brown-stained paper cups. She looked up at Bekali, mostly with her eyes, her head reluctant to stretch.

'But you reckon they coulda been though.'

'Could've been. Anyone could be a Lemon, they say. Maybe you.'

'You can relax, burger lady.' Bekali rolled a few chewed pencils back and forth on the desk. 'I'm no Lemon.'

'Yeah, but I don't know that, do I? You see?'

Bekali shuffled along concrete embankment of the canal. She watched the litter lazily overtake her on the oily water. She unwrapped her blue bubblegum. Chew, blow, pop. She rolled the thoughts in her head; they ground like worry balls and made her teeth clench. Whispers and rumours of the Lemons were spreading faster than she could sleuth out the facts. The sun fell back over the horizon and sent her shadow streaming ahead of her and into the canal.

Over next breakfast, the low white morning burned her eyes. She opened the morning newspaper under her squinting, furrowed face. 'Records Show Greatest Rise in Promotions Among Blondes,' the headline screamed. She spooned floppy, milky cornflakes into her mouth. 'Could the Boom in Blondes Reveal the Lemons at Last?' said page four. Could it?

Midday found her lying back on a stiff bed at the Aaron Street brothel, staring out at the earth-patterned wallpaper that burned in the sunlight that came pouring through the thin, red curtains. The friendly prostitutes, who had long envied her sleuthing adventures, sat on the four corners of the bed in pyjamas and pink rollers. The brothel on Aaron Street was frequented by many a powerful person and Bekali knew the place well. The prostitutes leaned in to tell their stories; the bedsprings shifted. Creakity, creak.

'Oh, we see alls kinds of suited types in here,' said Anehita, her unnaturally long eyelashes slashing tiger stripes of mascara on to her high cheeks. She leaned back against the wall, arms crossed over her plump torso, satisfied by her insider knowledge.

'Them blondes sure have been in the thicks of it,' said Roxana with excitement, her rollers shaking lose from her hair. They bounced off her pointed hips and scattered to the floor but she ignored them and lay forwards on the bed, resting her chin on her wrists.

'Sure, they are! Just last week one of thems tried to lay his hand to Roxana,' said Fareeza, touching her heart and pressing into the soft flesh of her bare bosom. She crossed her legs and pulled her hair back to a bun. 'And that other blond guy went to leave without payin', remember?'

'Oh yeah. And the stinkin' perve boy – was he blond too?' asked Naheed, trying to roll up her tights without laddering them on her diamond nails. Her lips were lined in black and her hair was as long as her back, tumbling like a waterfall over her tattoos.

'Oh, I think he was,' said Anehita. 'He definitely was.'

'We shouldn't be lettin' 'em back,' said Roxana, kicking her legs up so her feet rested over the frilly knickers veiling her behind.

'Nuh-uh! Too much trouble, them Lemons!' said Fareeza, fiddling impatiently with her bra until both nipples were poking through the holes in the cups.

And Bekali lay among the prostitutes. Her body rocked as they leaned across the bed to swap tales, laugh and bitch. They beautified their bodies for the night ahead with powders and creams and oil; their chosen scents waltzed through the air and blended to a sharp mist. Underwear was swapped and fought over; shoes were chosen and dismissed. And throughout, all kinds of nasty tales seeped out, almost all of them involving a blond, as far as they could recall. Bekali wondered, her red eyes streaming from a mis-shot sprig of perfume, how deep the blond Lemons had managed to root themselves.

Skipping through the main plaza of the city, Bekali was drawn to the large screen leering over the square. Two newsfolk were discussing Lemons in the army. Had the presence of blondes in the Barium Bridge Massacre been significant? Would fewer innocent lives been lost at war without Lemons in the ranks? Should they remove blondes from service? Question, question, question. No answers. Not yet.

Bekali's pupils dilated fat under the screen. It looked back at her. She may well be the go-to sleuth for carving through the city's underbelly but, this time, she was merely one among the millions across the country looking for Mrs Lemon. What was her forte?

It was then that she remembered an old friend. A faithful friend from years back. She walked the gravelled edge of the rusted railroad that ran from the city's heart to the outskirts, where the grass still tried to grow. She swept between endless rows of grey brick houses on roads optimistically named for plant life, and the distant electricity of the city let the sky lie blue. Hyacinth Avenue. But no hyacinths in sight.

She struck the wide, white, wooden door. Thud, thud, thud. Azeta first peeked through the crack of the doorway, then welcomed her inside, a smile splitting her face. Her hair, once light, was oil-black, wet and tied on top of her head. Black dye rolled over Azeta's neck, bleeding into brown finger-streaks on her shoulders.

'Bekali! Bekali, oh, it has been so long!' Azeta chirped. She continually tightened and tucked the towel around her chest. She was far too slight of frame for the towel to hold itself around her.

'You've gone and dyed your 'air, Azeta,' Bekali noted, thieving a praline from the open chocolate box on the table. Azeta put a pan of water on to boil. It rocked a metallic prattle on the uneven hob.

'There's a lot of bad words out there for people with hair like mine. Best to darken up a bit 'til it all dies down, I say.' She put out two mugs: pot, pot.

'So, what's the deal with your blondeness, then?' Bekali asked.

'I'm just blonde, Bekali. I don't know about other blondes, much, but I've always been blonde and know no more about it.'

'You a Lemon, then?'

'I don't know any Lemons in my family,' Azeta tucked her towel under her armpits. 'Trust me now – I went n' looked. Was plannin' to blot 'em out of the family tree if I found 'em.' She smiled, for an instant. She dropped a mesh ball of tea leaves into the pan. 'You're not here for me are you? Friends first right?'

'Friends first. I ain't got no trouble with you, Azeta.'

And that was that. They spent the rest of their day over tea, recanting the old days, before adulthood had brought them troubles and responsibility. Azeta stood an arch over the bath, smoking a damp cigarette, while Bekali rinsed her hair clean. She spoke of the days when they used to steal away to dance in bars, scrawl and share poems in tatty, ring-bound notepads, and scrounge tobacco from midnight taxi drivers.

Another night tarred the day dark. Bekali walked between the market stalls. Boys and girls shouted headlines from their stacks of rags.

'Blondes Take Your Jobs!'

'Will Lemons Push Us Out? Read About It!'

'Do You Have Lemon Genes? The Truth Inside!'

The city was abuzz with unrest. Bekali prowled the shade of the rooftops, looking down. Blondes were being shoved by heavy hands. She saw butchers came from behind their meat to shout at a couple of passing blonde bankers, who ducked and jogged on. The butchers swished their bloody cleavers threateningly. Swish, swish, spatter.

It got worse. From her high, hidden perches she saw blonde children kicked and tripped to puddles by the other kids. A building wave of anger and paranoia turned ordinary people to a fury; gangs of everyday folk had taken to pulling those with dark hair and fair skin to the ground. They'd hold 'em tight and tear their clothes away to check their bodies to see if they were really dark haired. They usually were. Bekali thought of Azeta. She wondered if this malice had always lived within her citizenry.

Eventually, to quell an environment of escalating bloodshed, the government gathered up all the blondes and separated them from the dark-haired folk. Clink, clink, clink. The prisons locked. But now they had a great cluster of blondes and no further ideas. This was a great source of consternation for the nation: the prisons were full and the blondes now were being fed and cared for by the cash-strapped people of Grimoire. Debates sprang up across the media. Bekali watched it all on the TV. She pulled herself into the armchair and grabbed her knees; the cold glare of the TV caught the mascara dripping over her face. Flash, flash. The colours on the screen changed.

Bekali watched the rich and dark-haired sit around a studio table, arguing over how to deal with the ensnared blondes. One of them – a stylish man with a curl of a fringe – fired out his own idea with a red-faced conviction.

See, the Xacta Project was nearly complete. Finally a Grimoirian would walk on the moon. It had taken decades of delay and mountains of money, so the anticipation was feverish. The man on TV made it sound so obvious. Load the Lemons onto the Xacta rocketship and send them all to the moon. Why, if they wanted to be an important part of Grimoire, then so be it. Of course, they'd have to stay on the moon. They couldn't return with the astronauts.

The audience clapped and cheered. Bekali silenced her television. She sat in the dark. Her heart pricked her nerves. The people had applauded. Bekali let her hands meet in slow, deliberate melancholy. Clap. Clap. Clap.

And so it was that she found herself back under the high cirrus of cigar smoke in the office of Mr Saaed. She sat in the oak and leather swivel chair, opposite Mr Saaed's walnut and fur throne. She allowed the full length of her limbs to hold wide and rigid over the contours of the chair.

'So, I ain't found that Mrs Lemon,' Bekali scratched the oak arms lightly with her nails. Scratch, scratch, scratch.

'That there is a shame,' Mr Saaed purred over his cigar. His words tangled in the smoke. 'I heard you were the best.'

'No. You knew I was the best. Didn' ya?' Scratch, scratch.

Mr Saaed smiled, his cigar pointed erect.

'You know what makes me so good?' said Bekali.

'I do.'

'I know everyone, all the cracks, all the corners – you remember. I'm the perfect tool for finding needles in haystacks.'

'Or placing needles in haystacks.' The cigar glowed.

A pause. A puff of smoke.

'There ain't no Mrs Lemon, is there?'

Mr Saaed turned to the large window, to the galaxy of city lights. 'Oh, there is now. In their minds, there is. That's all that matters, isn't it?'

'But all those people...'

'There are too many people. Far too many people for us to bear. But you can't rid yourself of half the people unless you have the other half behind you. Why, we'd look like monsters.' Mr Saaed's hot ash spilled onto the floor. 'Best to let them construct their own enemy.'

'I'll tell ev'ryone...'

'You won't get this out of their heads now. Easy to light a match, isn't it? Not so simple to snuff out a bushfire. Besides...'

But then the sky was alight. Bekali and Mr Saaed were lit from the window as a fiery shape burst from the horizon. A white rainbow. It arced over the city, united in celebration. It rose high into the sky.

Inside, a heroic team of astronauts and a cityful of blondes. Above, a waxing moon looked down with a welcoming smile.

Mrs Lemon's Children

The Meanest and the Modest

In a tiny indistinct smudge, hidden in the depths of the universe, there was a small swirling galaxy. At the end of one of its great, sparkling arms, an inconsiderable star glowed yellow. And, hidden in the orbit of that star was a tiny planet, warmed by the proximity of the starlight. A minor part of that planet was covered in solid ground. And on the least deadly parts of that land, small creatures that called themselves humans blinked in and out of existence, briefly considering themselves masters of the universe.

These humans learned to pass their knowledge from generation to generation, and so they sat proudly on centuries of cumulative exploration, manifested in plastics, lights and monuments. They clouded as a hive across the full circumference of the planet, linked to one another by an electronic era of communication. Their knowledge filled thousands of libraries and spilled from their books onto screens and into disks. They had buttons and switches that could easily change their civilisation and ecology in two blinks of an eye; such was the connection they shared.

One day, their activity – which consisted mainly of shifting imaginary figures between computers – was interrupted by a large, blinking machine, as red and bulbous as a tomato and as large as a hotel, drifting from the sky like a dying balloon. It perched on a snow-decked mountain clinging to the rock with a hundred spindly, brass legs. The human population looked up on this bizarre, visiting construction with the piqued hodge-podge of emotion that you might imagine for such an unexpected guest.

The visitor did not stay silent. It spoke out to all the world, speaking to every last being in every language that had ever been uttered, so that all would understand its purpose.

'Earth of grass and water. We are travellers who journey the vastness of space, collecting knowledge and pursuing discovery. We have seen your planet to be one of the few fortunate enough to spawn life and we seek council with you to discuss how we might benefit one another. We see that you are many; too many to speak at once, so we ask that you send a single representative to convene with us.'

Then silence.

What excitement! What anticipation! What could be gleaned from these strange travellers? And who on Earth should they send?

Naturally, the leaders of the world took it upon themselves to gather for serious discussion in a secret gunmetal room under the sea. They sat around a circular table so vast that those opposite one another could barely hear each other's words. The table was laid with many varieties of bottled water and glasses that twinkled with the lights and screens that surrounded them. Present at the table were moustaches, bobs, hats, crosses, crescents, suits, robes and dresses, each looking at the others with suspicious, twitching brows. This was an opportunity for a great many of them, and a potential catastrophe for others.

A bespectacled lady began the discussion. 'Has anyone had any thoughts as to the ambassador we should send?'

A very tall man in a very tight suit criss-crossed his fingers before him and said, 'Clearly we should send the greatest of us – the most powerful leader at the table. One who can speak for all of us.'

'But who is the most powerful of us?' said a large-eyed woman, bearing a sceptre. 'You think it is you? Ha! I oversee twice the land you do!'

'But I trade three times the quantities of your country!' said the tall man in the tight suit. 'Why, almost all of you use our exports.'

'Fools!' said a long-bearded leader. 'My country has twice the people of both of yours together! I represent far more people than anyone!'

And so a loud squabble broke out around the round table. Everybody had a case to make, but no one could agree on the measure of importance. The bespectacled lady silenced them.

'We will never come to an agreement like this, Ladies, Gentleman and President Trebor. We need to agree on a selection method, free from bias. Any ideas?'

'How about a lottery?' said a very short man in very large heels. 'Give everyone in the world one ticket and give each of them a fair chance at being our ambassador.'

'And risk sending some crazy fool to speak for the world?' spluttered a woman, whose dark hair was scraped back in a severe bun. 'Not a chance! I'd rather send my ex-husband!'

Everybody fell silent, except for a white-bearded man, who laughed long and loud while the others fidgeted and pondered. A bald man with thin sideburns absently rolled a shiny coin in his long fingers.

'An auction!' said a red-suited woman, pointing a finger. 'The honour should go to the highest bidder!'

'Yes indeed!' said a long-necked man, slamming a large purse onto the round table. 'I call one hundred million for myself!'

'Two hundred million!' yelled the long-bearded leader.

'And to whom is this money to be paid?' asked the bespectacled lady.

'Why, to the second highest bidder,' said the long-necked man.

And, all around the table, there was shouting and waving of notes and pushing back and forth of gold as the delegates offered riches and trades and legislation, puffing out their chests and banging their fists against the table.

'Let us not be so foolish!' said a man with a button-threatening belly. 'Most of us cannot afford to play a part in your frivolous money games!'

And so the shouting ceased and the red-faced traders sat down again, straightening their excitement-ruffled clothing. It was beginning to seem as if this wouldn't be sorted in time for tea.

The very short man in very large heels spoke with a soft squeak. 'I think, still, we should try to be fair.' He stammered a little as he spoke. 'We should find the person who embodies all of the qualities of all the people on Earth. The most average of us.'

There was much muttering and nodding among the table's occupants. They should definitely try to be fair. Definitely try.

'But how do we find this person, or even know what he will be like?' asked a white man in a black shirt.

'Ah, I think I can help with that,' said a woman with pointed cheek bones. 'We have a super computer that collects personal information for everybody across the world. For security, of course.'

Of course, they all muttered. Much was done for the purpose of security. And how thankful they were for it now: how excellent; how useful.

The high cheek-boned woman continued. 'All that needs to be done is to ask the machine to find the average person from all the people stored in its population memory banks. Then we can simply collect that person and bring them here to meet the visitors.'

So they wheeled in the great machine and asked it to find the most average person in all of humanity. The machine sat, a great twist of metal and plastic, whirring and flashing magnificently within its stillness. Hours ticked by as it endeavoured to process all of humankind at once – its greatest ever task. Several times the machine juddered and hissed as if disgruntled at its laborious servitude. The President of Iceland was seated nearest the machine so he took charge of jiggling the mouse every few minutes to stop the screensaver kicking in.

After much hard work, the great machine did eventually slow to a conclusion, announcing its completion with a satisfying ping.

'Tell us – what does it say?' asked a King with veiny temples.

'The machine has flagged our average person,' said the woman with the pointed cheek bones.

'And who is it?' asked the white-bearded man. 'Tell us!'

'Her name is Qiao Kapoor. She is intersex – born with both male and female genitals. She is a lady of dual nationality – her father is Indian and her mother Chinese. She is missing part of an arm, due to an accident in childhood. She sells goods at her local market for a living, and is a bisexual atheist.'

There was the briefest moment of silence in the room that hit the room like a big, fat semicolon. Then, activity resumed, twice as loudly as before.

'What?' a woman in a long pencil skirt shouted. 'What is this? A woman with all the genitals?'

'And an atheist?' cried a Prince in a round scarf. 'How can our ambassador be an atheist when almost everyone believes in God?'

The bony-cheeked woman paced, shuffling through her notes. 'You are almost correct – people believe in a god, but there is much disagreement about which God. If they believe in one god, their belief in all other gods is zero. When that's all averaged out, every individual god ends up with a very low belief score and so the machine has chosen an atheist, who also has little belief in any particular god.'

'This is a preposterousness!' said a man in a colourful beret. 'How can we send this ugly mess of a woman to represent us all?'

The bony-cheeked woman argued, 'she represents a little bit of everyone, just as you asked!'

'She represents no one!' said a woman with fierce shoulder pads. 'She is a uniquity!'

'Her sexuality is disturbing,' said a man with a loosened tie. 'How will the visitors understand the way normal people pair off? This is all wrong.'

'Disturbing is right!' said a heart-faced lady. 'Disgusting is more accurate! I say, be gone with her!'

So, they had returned to where they started, with the table reduced to silent, angry pondering. Water glasses rose and fell like pistons.

'We are going about this all wrong,' said a man with a beard, but no moustache. 'There are many averages. Searching for the mean of society meant we were always bound to find a patchwork person that, in actuality, sits far, far from any of us.' The man rubbed the bones of his nose. 'We must, instead, discover the *mode* of the people to find the one that represents our most abundant qualities. Someone we can relate to.'

Yes, yes, yes, they all agreed. This person – the mode of humankind - would be a one-person democracy. They cranked the machine once more, with greater enthusiasm. While it hummed and juddered, some played cards, others exchanged anecdotes, and the President of Iceland continued to jiggle the mouse when it struggled. And, once again, the satisfying ping signalled the machine's conclusion.

'What does it say? Pray, tell us!' asked a woman with long curls.

The woman with the bony cheeks read from the machine: 'It's a woman,' she said. 'A Chinese woman named Ai Emma Li.'

There was some frowning around the table.

'She is middle-aged, Christian, heterosexual, married and has a full complement of limbs,' the bony-cheeked woman continued.

From the mouths, once weighted with frowns, came pitch-turning grunts of approval.

'She lives in a shanty town in a Chinese city. She is very, very poor.'

'Well, then, let's summon her!' a very large man with blue-rimmed glasses said. His fingers drummed on his shirted belly.

And so Ai Emma Li was brought to the gunmetal room of the round table. She was very nervous, but understood enough English to nod along to those around the table. They sat her down and offered her water and tea and sandwiches, and continued to tell her how important she was. How she had been selected. They asked her no questions: not of her background, her family or her politics. Instead, they made it their mission to inform her about the wider world as they saw it. What mattered most to the globe; what the people were sure to wish for from the visitors; what they would want her to convey; what to ask for; how to act; what to wear...

Ai Emma Li sat as politely as she could, keeping her knees together and her hands resting gently on them. She tightened her lips before she was asked a question and followed her days of grooming and training as best she could. She tried to follow the speech training, the art of negotiation and the importance of etiquette and first impressions. She sat silently while those around the table argued over all manner of small details, like whether she should be dressed in many colours or plainly suited; whether she should ask for energy, knowledge or weaponry; what they should offer in return.

Ai Emma Li had never before concerned herself with such grand matters. Her life, for the most part, considered only the momentum of her family's upkeep. The ideas being discussed around her were so much grander than she had ever known and she wondered why she, of all people, had been chosen as the tiny voice of such tremendous affairs.

The delegates around the table were finally satisfied that Ai Emma Li knew everything she had to do and say for the benefit of humankind. They informed the rest of the world that they had chosen her to speak to the visitors on their behalf – she was, they proclaimed confidently, someone who embodied the majority. Many citizens baulked and raged at their lack of consultation, but the circle of leaders knew they would never find a person better suited to represent them all, and certainly no one who wouldn't cause even more anger. They packed a big, fat-wheeled car and sent Ai Emma Li up the mountain to convene with the great, red machine that had come from the stars. The journey was long and Ai Emma Li felt her hips bruising as she was knocked from side to side inside the vehicle, but she stayed quiet.

But as the car neared the great, red machine, the booming, multi-lingual voice rang out across the world once more:

'We thank you for visiting us. We were very much impressed by your envoy. She was incredibly illuminating.'

What was this? Who had broken through the ranks of soldiers guarding the landing site? Who had visited the visitors? And what on Earth had they said?

'Thank you for informing us that your planet is full of delicious, delicious oil. As a token of our gratitude, we shall of course grant your one, worthy wish, as promised to Qiao Kapoor.'

The leaders at the circular table were mystified. All, except for the woman with the pointed cheek bones, who sat back in her chair and sighed a long and ragged breath. The round table's ferocity towards poor Qiao Kapoor had infuriated her. She had used her powers to secrete Qiao Kapoor away, up the mountain to the great, red machine before the round table could send another envoy in her place.

The leaders watched in horror as the great, red vehicle lifted into the air, leaving Qiao Kapoor on the mountain, waving a friendly goodbye. The red machine hopped across the Earth and sucked all of the black oil from beneath the land and sea with juicy, slurpy abandon as the leaders of the round table sat in despair, burying their faces in their fingers.

Satisfied with its harvest, the red machine rose into the air and away to the stars once more. And just as the ship travelled beyond sight, rainbows fell from the sky. A technicolour blizzard sank from the heavens; tiny rainbows drifted to every man, woman and child on Earth. The rainbows swallowed their thoughts, their colours and their shapes and blended to a great swirling tornado of colour that brought together all the elements of all the people of the world.

And then the great rainbow uncurled. All the qualities of all the people were scattered at random among all of humanity, so that now everyone was as mixed and colourful as Qiao Kapoor, the mean, patchwork person. And they looked upon themselves and each other and saw they were anew.

Billions of brand new people stood where the old ones had once been, each without allegiance, bias or indoctrination. Their faces and body bore a random, florid mix of all the people they replaced. Their minds contained fractures of the ideas, personalities and quirks of a billion others. They shared in their differences and no person was as they were before. And so they owned nothing, owed nothing and knew nothing.

So they started again.

Author's Note

This book grew from a realisation I had at the coincidence of a few of my interests: scepticism, science and the media. The pursuit of truth is a fascinating and noble endeavour and has allowed us as a species to distinguish ourselves from other animals in a way previously unseen. Our brains are incredibly powerful tools that can imagine, calculate, reason, emote and control and, consequently, we forget their limitations.

A good scientist and a good sceptic will endeavour never to forget the limitations of the human brain – its strange attachment to coincidence, its emotional bias, its complete inability to grasp statistics. It's so easy to jump to conclusions based on preconceived ideas, even if you genuinely think you are being balanced and clearing your mind of bias. It is in our nature to spot patterns, connect dots and categorise people and situations into little boxes that or so hard to change once they are in our mind.

The media exploit and fall victim to this in a massive, massive way. In Britain, most headlines are built upon the readers' preconceived notions about the subjects of the articles. The words, 'Muslims', 'immigrants', 'tax', 'romp', 'BBC', 'hate', 'Diana' and 'quango', for example, immediately strike something deep in the heart of the reader, based on years of previous narrative. The news has become something of a soap opera, where all the characters are meticulously planted seeds that have been watered and cultured by the media.

Why do I bring up the media, then? Because it works. Even the flimsiest of stories has a devastating impact, because the power of the story is greater than the power of *fact*. If a front page news article runs with a 'Scandal in Climate Change Camp', based on the most ridiculous premise, that article will do more damage than can be repaired by the thirty years of climate change data available at the click of mouse.

Scepticism and science and fact can be dry and dull. It can be complicated and hard work. Often, there is no black and white answer. Often, you have to think about it, or decide not to come to a conclusion until you are able to investigate further. It can be frustrating, and that's not an easy thing to deal with without a decent amount of training and patience.

But a story – oh, how a story can work wonders!

So why not some stories about science and scepticism, feminism and human rights, society and philosophy? Why not rekindle the old magic of the fairy tale to allow people to see how characters react in difficult situations and what happens if they don't think with a critical mind?

That was the experiment. I hope you enjoyed it.

Acknowledgements

My awesome wife, Lauren Taylor, encouraged me throughout this endeavour and ruthlessly edited the first few drafts of this anthology with the ferocity that only a wife could give. The brilliant Lauren Jessup was kind enough to give me her sceptical and personal thoughts. Christine Blachford monstered over the manuscript as only a writer could – she, Nik Johnson, Rebecca Tonks and Hannah Riggott are my writing buddies-in-arms.

Lorrie Hartshorn acted as editorial consultant on the final draft and did a brilliant job, though we will never see eye-to-eye on the word 'till'.

Satah Cameron, Stephenie Zvan, the aforementioned Rebecca Tonks and the quite, quite excellent *Trans Media Watch* offered important guidance in particular subjects where I was concerned of my ignorance.

Thank you, Deja Whitehouse, for rekindling me with my love of writing.

Thank you to the illustrators who collaborated on this with me – you're all awesome.

I feel particularly enlightened in the subjects explored in this book by the following people, in no particular order: Richard Dawkins, Matt Dillahunty and the Atheist Experience, Steve Novella and the Skeptics' Guide the Universe, The Godless Bitches, Rebecca Watson and Skepchick, The F Word, Trans Media Watch, Greta Christina, Steve Baxter, and Kevin Arscott.

My friends are some of the most honest, encouraging, creative and intelligent people I will ever have the good fortune to know and I hope they enjoy this book, even a little bit.

Finally, Mum and Dad. They always stood by me, no matter what I wanted to do. Even when I scared the shit out of Dad when I thought I was going to do an art degree.

Illustrators

Cloe Ashton is an artist and skeptic whose art and blog can be viewed at www.obviouslycloe.com. She produces content for the scepticism/art fusion website, *Mad Art Lab*. Cloe illustrated *The Immortal*.

Fred Crawley is an artist and writer who creates fictional monster battles at *Zoo Fights* (zoofights.squarespace.com). Fred illustrated *The Pommasaurus Problem*.

Lauren Little is an illustrator and writer whose work can be found at www.laurenlittleillustration.com. She produces content for the scepticism/art fusion website, *Mad Art Lab*. Lauren illustrated *Hukommelsey* and *The Le Jambon Effect*.

Drew Mokris is one half of the team behind the webcomic *Left Handed Toons* (lefthandedtoons.com). He also produces music videos and animations at spinnerdisc.com. Drew illustrated *On a Hypotenuse*.

Heledd Straker is trained in fine art and the history thereof, has an MBA and works as a consultant. Heledd illustrated *Stained Glass Windows*.

Stuart F Taylor wrote these stories and illustrated all those not listed above. He is addicted to Copic markers.